Frogs, Floods and Fraud

The Tenacious Librarian Series

M K Scott

Frogs, Floods and Fraud

M K Scott

Copyright © 2023

Print Edition

Chapter One

THE AUTUMN AFTERNOON sun slipped through the parted gingham curtains, warming the late lunch crowd and those who chose to indulge themselves with one of Almost Home Café's delectable desserts. Silverware clattered against sturdy stoneware plates as customers gorged themselves on chicken fried steak, apple dumplings, and local gossip. Even when a person chose not to pass along idle chatter and rumors, it failed to stop ears from hearing. Tenny, Emerson's newest resident and official bookmobile owner, picked up her fork and used it to test the flakiness of her apple dumpling. After her Aunt Cinnamon passed, the thirty-ish former reference librarian found herself comparing every morsel she consumed to the delicious dishes her aunt made. Her aunt's award-winning cinnamon rolls earned her aunt her nickname. Cinnamon had even contributed desserts to the café. Although no other cooks even came close, the crust on the dumpling did flake nicely. She speared a bite, sampled it, swallowed, and sighed. "This is really good. Did they get someone new in the kitchen?"

Blue, Tenny's best friend and current companion, tucked a lock of her chin-length blonde hair behind her ear. "You bet. Otherwise, I wouldn't have suggested dropping in for a treat." She patted a rounded hip. "I can't afford any wasted calories on a tasteless concoction. Heard it was Philomena's grandson. You probably don't remember him. He was about ten years behind us in school, which makes him about twenty-two now."

"Whoever it is, he knows his way around a pastry cutter." Tenny loaded her fork with the glistening apples and feather-light crust. Her nose scrunched up and she lowered her fork to her plate, the delicious forkful uneaten at the first hint of overheard nasty gossip since it contained her first name.

The woman's voice carried loud enough for everyone in the small diner to hear. "I'm just saying, Dallas only went out with Tenny out of pity, ya know? With her aunt dying and all. Trust me, I have the details."

Blue reached across the table, nudging her friend's arm. "Ignore her. Shadow's only carrying out Rita's bidding. As far as Dallas dating people to cheer them up, you'd be the first." She smirked and then winked.

"Yeah." If anyone should know the machinations of the town's self-appointed queen, Tenny should—especially since she' stepped out with the queen's ex enough times to cause speculation. Once, a new girl showed up at school named Rita, wearing a necklace with her name on it. The story was that hometown Rita snatched the necklace off the girl and declared she couldn't use the name since it had already been taken and the town could only have one Rita. As for the girl, she disappeared. Maybe country life wasn't for her family. Shortly after that, Rita showed up wearing a silver necklace with her name in cursive script.

That's the type of person she was dealing with. While she wanted to chalk it up to malicious gossip, it did make her wonder. *What if Dallas only asked her out of kindness?* "Ah, let's talk about something else."

"Ready to do your first bookmobile run?" Blue asked as she finished up her apple dumpling and gave Tenny's uneaten portion a speculative glance.

Noticing her gaze, Tenny pulled the plate closer. "I intend to finish it, even if I do it at home." She inhaled deeply and then spoke. "As for the first run, technically I'm ready, but…" She sucked in her lips and shook her head. "…I'm a little worried. Sure, I know this was my aunt's dream and all. I'm not even all that good at driving an extra-long van, especially on all those narrow, winding country roads."

"Practice." Blue bobbed her chin with a touch of certainty. "We'll take the bookmobile for a dry run of sorts."

Before she could ask for more details, their server swung by with a coffee carafe and topped off their cups. The server, a middle-aged woman sporting gray streaks that resembled the zig zags in the Bride of Frankenstein's hairdo, or at least it drew that comparison around Halloween, delivered food and drink with a side of chatter. "Did you hear," she started, "that Rivertown has to move? Turns out flood insurance stops paying out after so many floods. Personally," she propped her free hand on her waist as if settling in for a lengthy conversation, "they should have called the place *Floodsville*." She barked with laughter at her own comment. No one else chuckled.

Tenny noted her friend's furrowed brow and pinched lips and then remembered. "Don't you have relatives in Rivertown?"

"Yes." The normally gregarious Blue's one-word answer hinted at much more, better told in another place.

Not deterred by the monosyllabic response, the server cleared her throat and added, "You had better get the spare room cleaned out because you're probably having company."

Both Blue and Tenny shot each other befuddled looks before turning back to their waitress. "Um…" Tenny tried to remember her name and then noticed her neatly printed name tag. "…Sally. Are you doing psychic readings along with delivering pie?"

"Ha! Ha!" She barked out the laugh. "I don't remember you being funny, but people change, I suppose." Sally pursed her lips as if she doubted the possibility of Tenny ever coming up with a funny or two.

It didn't seem like that needed a comment, but she did need to know where Sally was going with her conversation. When it came to getting information, Blue usually jumped in feet first, but not today. This morning it would be up to Tenny. "How did you get all this information? Online?"

"Mercy, no. You can't believe what all these kids are putting online. They make up half of that stuff. My second cousin married a man from Rivertown. He's got people there." She leaned forward and put up a flattened hand to the side of her mouth as if to shield her words from possible lip readers. "Story is, the town council presented its case to both the state and federal governments for assistance in moving higher up. They both ponied up some funds. I even heard the self-appointed mayor started a Go Fund Me account on the Internet that raised a lot. Anyhow, everything was falling into place. Seems like folks felt sorry for Rivertown's citizens—people contributing twenty dollars, sometimes fifty. One big spender even gave thousands. So much money. Heard it was millions. Basically, from strangers with no stake in Rivertown." A sigh and then a head wag announced Sally's feelings. She lowered her voice. "Then the money from all that online begging just vanished!" She placed the coffee carafe on the table and snapped her fingers. "Like that. It's gone! That's why I said you'd better plan on company. I imagine your relatives will be headed this way soon."

A town moving should be relatively big news, but a town losing all its money in one fell swoop should be even bigger news. Odd she hadn't heard about it. To be fair, she hadn't been watching the news due to spending all her time fixing up the bookmobile. "How come I haven't heard of this?"

Using three fingers, Sally tapped her own chest. "*I* just found out about it. No worries. As soon as they catch that Jess Singleton, they'll have their money back."

"Jess?" A paler than usual Blue squeaked out the name.

"Yep!" Sally concurred. "The money vanished about the same time she did. It had to be her."

A customer behind them grumbled, "What does a person have to do to get a cup of coffee around here?"

Sally sniffed and picked up the carafe while muttering, "Some people."

"Okay." Grateful for the interruption, Tenny stood, scooping up her apple dumpling. "I'm going to get a box for this and pay. We're getting out of here. I'll meet you outside."

Blue wordlessly exited the booth and diner. Weird, her normally perky friend went all moody and silent. She read once on a T-shirt that good friends are ones who help you hide the body. Nope. Good friends are the ones who help you turn an aging camper van into a bookmobile, which required much more work than hiding a body. It was her turn to be the supportive friend. After what felt like twenty minutes, Sally took her money and boxed her dessert while implying that Tenny should eat more pie to fill out her skinny frame.

Bolting out the door with her to-go box in hand, she spotted Blue texting on her phone next to a dusty pickup truck. A few long strides brought her abreast of her friend. "What's up?"

Blue glanced up, bit her bottom lip, and then spoke. "You know that Jess is my cousin." She stomped one foot. "I know for a fact she wouldn't have taken the money. As for vanishing, I'm not surprised. That's been her only goal in life—to leave Rivertown. We *have* to find her. She has no clue she's being framed for a crime." She brandished her phone. "She's not replying to my texts either. We have to do something!" Sure, her bestie's wide eyes and climbing color denoted her outrage, but Blue stayed loyal to the end. Maybe her cousin helped herself to the funds, or maybe she didn't. A good friend would help clear the cousin's name until it became obvious Jess was as dirty as a pig in a mud puddle. "Why not make our bookmobile dry run to Rivertown? That way we might unearth some actual facts as opposed to relying on Sally's questionable tales from her cousin."

Chapter Two

T HE BOOKMOBILE WAITED in front of Tenny's house as the two women crunched through fallen leaves, planning their fact-finding mission and enjoying the respite from the summer heat and humidity. The side of the vehicle depicted children reading outside on a green, grassy slope and the blue sky coming alive with dragons, horses, and mythical characters. Even though she received a generous inheritance and stock portfolio, Tenny's financial strategy included dipping into it as little as possible. So far, she didn't have a clear idea about how much money would be needed to make the bookmobile business self-sustaining. A smile stretched across her face as she took in the professional wrap mural done for the bookmobile—so totally worth it.

Technically, Tenny could have parked it in the narrow driveway on the side of the house, but that meant backing up all the way to the road. At this point in her bus driving experience, she avoided anything tricky, such as backing up or parallel parking with anything larger than her subcompact car. Roundabouts designed for smaller vehicles could prove difficult, or they would if Emerson had any. "Do you think the way to Rivertown will be a straight shot?"

Blue stopped walking and directed a curious look at Tenny, who also halted. Her eyebrows arched as she asked, "You're not afraid of driving?"

"I don't know." She swallowed and then tapped two fingers on her lips before answering. "I've driven up and down the roads here. Let's face it, we almost *never* get traffic. What will I do if I run into a combine?" Around harvest time, combines, mammoth tractors, and semis packed full of grain crowded the roads. Anyone in a normal sized vehicle darted into a nearby driveway or backed off the road.

"Same thing you'd do if you were in your car. For Pete's sake, it's just an extra-long van. You're more like a soccer mom than a cross-the-road trucker."

"You're right," Tenny half-heartedly agreed as they drew closer to the bookmobile. "I have a longer than average learning curve. However, once I learn how to do something, I'm okay."

Her friend had calmed her down when her actual intention was to ease Blue's anxiety. Blue and her husband, Griffin, ran a small dairy called Moo Town. The day-to-day operations fell to the couple with some seasonal help. "Won't you need to be back in time for second milking?"

"Nope." Blue managed a grin with the word. "Strangely, after our ruckus with Rupert being cow-napped, Griffin decided we needed more dependable help with the girls."

Most of the locals knew when Blue referred to the *girls*, she meant their dairy cows. As a couple with no children, they doted on their cows, naming each one of them, and claimed they had specific personalities. This made the idea of hiring outside help surprising. "Griffin is okay with outside help now. He's doing background checks on potential employees online. It cost about thirty dollars, but you'd be amazed at all the stuff you can discover. To tell the truth, I'm glad I have some free time. Sure, it's supposed to be spent writing advertising for our dairy shop." She grimaced, then shrugged. "Today though, I need to get ahold of Jess. She's about ten years younger than me. I remember back when she was twelve, and she confided her goal to leave Rivertown. As far as I know, her goal never changed."

Even though Tenny knew her friend tended to side with the underdog, she felt the need to point out the obvious. "I imagine she could get very far away with all that money."

"Shame on you!" Blue delivered a smart rap to Tenny's arm. "You're talking about family."

"What about Rufus, who took a hay baler for a joy ride through town and ended up parking it inside the front wall of the IGA grocery?"

"Rufus is *Griffin's* family. I always said my hubby was the pick of the litter. I know Jess. She has a good heart." She crossed both arms and pursed her lips. "I know you don't know her. When she was sixteen, around Christmas time, a neighbor's house burned down. At the time, she'd been working at the local fast food joint, saving money for a car. Once she heard the family wouldn't have any Christmas, she withdrew her money from her savings account and bought them presents. Even bought them groceries, too. She borrowed her dad's truck and delivered them anonymously on Christmas Eve."

"How do you know about that?"

"Her father told me. Come on, parents are never as unaware as kids think they are." She parked one hand on her hip. "Does that sound like someone who would steal from their own town?"

"No." Tenny, a big fan of mystery novels and police dramas, knew often the least likely person often was the culprit. "Still, she could have changed. People do."

"Not that much. She once rescued a snapping turtle that was hit by a car. You know those turtles are as ugly as sin with a personality to match. Who would rescue such a creature, but a truly kind individual?"

On that note, a furry, masked face peeked out from the colorful mums lining the sidewalk to her aunt's house, which was now Tenny's. "You got me there. I certainly wouldn't nursemaid a snapping turtle." She directed her attention to the raccoon, Precious, that her aunt had raised from a kit and had inadvertently passed on to Tenny. "Not me. I wouldn't even take care of a hurt raccoon."

"Oh please." Blue gave her friend a slight shove. "I've seen you cook for Precious."

"It's not an everyday thing. Eventually, he's going to return to the woods and become a wild creature."

"You keep telling yourself that." Blue chuckled. "No way will he give up the sweet life. Enough about Precious. We need a reason to be in Rivertown, especially since I haven't been there in years. With everything that's happened, we will need to look like we haven't come by to gawk." Blue cocked her head, resembling a white silkie bantam chicken with her blonde hair ruffled by the breeze.

"How about we stopped by when we heard the news about your town and nothing cheers you up like a good book?"

"Has promise," Blue concurred. "I would have to say nothing cheers you up like getting the money back that was stolen from you. We need to stop by the farm and pick up Sir Moolah."

"Should I ask? Calf? Better yet, why would we take a cow—small or otherwise—with us?" Blue loved fancy names for the cows and Tenny hoped she didn't expect to push a calf into the newly furbished van.

"Oh, no. He's a stray pup I found when I went into Beechnut for new muck boots. He followed me around, looking so sad that I had to bring him home. Anyhow, he's a bayer and a howler, which doesn't agree with the girls. They produce sour milk. I think Griffin's words when I left were something about taking that creature with you. The two haven't bonded yet. I'm sure the pup would love a road trip."

"Oh, yeah," Tenny commented, but had her doubts. All she needed was a howling canine in her van as she traveled down unfamiliar roads, driving a vehicle triple the size of her car. "I see you and Jess have a lot in common when it comes to rescuing hard-luck cases."

Chapter Three

A LIGHT, UNEXPECTED drizzle pattered on the van roof, creating a slight echo. Tenny's lips pulled to one side as she carefully steered around another gaping hole in the road, muttering to herself, "When will they *actually* fix the road?"

Her companion, Blue, commented matter-of-factly, "You know the answer to that as well as I do. Probably in five years or more. Big cities get their roads fixed first." She flipped down the visor to block the sunbeams filtering through the raindrops. "The sun is shining while it rains. You know what that means."

Less than sold on their current road trip, Tenny mumbled her reply. "The devil is mad at his wife again."

"Please…" Blue stretched out the word for emphasis. "I prefer something more cheerful. Sun showers are good luck."

"Of course, they are. Why should I have expected otherwise from you?" Tenny managed a snort at her friend's determined optimism even if it meant twisting a few dated idioms to suit her own purpose. The white fences outlining green pastures and an oversized white dairy barn with *Moo Town* painted in bold, six-foot letters came into view as they neared Blue's property. Despite the fact that no other vehicles existed on the country lane, Tenny turned on her turn signal and braked gently for the turn. As she did so, she heard books slapping against books—exactly what she'd feared. The customized bookmobiles with locking shelf covers came with an astronomical price tag. Bungee cords might work if she had hooks on the shelves for attachment purposes. Twisting in her seat, she examined the filled but messy shelves behind her. There were no books on the floor, so all was good.

The tires clutched at the gravel and pulled the substantial vehicle up the hill. People who said books weren't heavy had never filled a bookmobile with them. She sucked in her lips, wondering if she should have paid for a professional refurbishing. Those bookmobile conversion companies charged a great deal. Besides, the money it took to finish out a simple van would serve her much better paying her bills and keeping the mobile library running.

Before they completed their rumble up the hill to Moo Town Dairy, a dog dashed from a half-open barn door. Spotting them, it erupted into a mournful howl, which resulted in a thirty-something man attired in a plaid flannel shirt and jeans, which he tucked into high rubber boots, stepping out with a less-than-pleased expression. "Oh no!" Blue inhaled audibly. "He's mad."

"The dog?" While Tenny liked other people's dogs, that made her no expert in translating the yips, barks, and howls, or determining their canine moods.

"Not him. The other male in my life. Griffin."

"How can you tell?" Griffin usually displayed the same upbeat attitude as his wife, but not as perky as Blue—then again, few people were. Even though Tenny harbored no goals as far as matrimony, if she did it would be a marriage like Griffin and Blue's. They fell in love as friends, then developed a loving supportive relationship that managed to overcome each other's idiosyncrasies. "He looks about the same to me."

"It's the hands on the hips." A groan escaped Blue. "Maybe Moolah was an impetuous decision."

"You think?" Tenny failed to hide her sarcasm as she slowed to a careful stop in the oversized gravel parking area. If people happened to be sitting in the back sipping tea, not a drop would have been spilt. However, it was probably illegal to conduct a tea party in a moving vehicle unless all participants were seat belted. As soon as the vehicle quit moving, Blue unlatched her safety belt, swung the door open, and ambled in the direction of her husband and dog.

The open door allowed Tenny to appreciate the sheer lung capacity of Sir Moolah. As a former reference librarian, she knew some dogs' barks started at 85 decibels and could get as loud as a motorcycle. Moolah's howl, while loud, possessed a certain musical quality to it as if harmonizing with a barbershop quartet. Blue pecked her husband on the cheek, scooped up the medium-size dog, murmured something undecipherable, and then climbed back into the bookmobile with her cargo. "Let's go!" she ordered and leaned back in her seat with a sigh.

"Is Griffin good?"

A choked snort laugh served as an initial answer before Blue elaborated. "Hope we're gone for hours. That's how long it will take for the girls to settle down."

Aware of Blue's need to mother all creatures, Tenny chose not to reply and concentrated on using the large parking lot to turn around. Thank goodness they had made the area big enough for supertankers that picked up the milk and took it to the bottling center. When Tenny pulled back onto the narrow county lane, she glanced over at the shaggy creature on Blue's lap. "Ah, what kind of dog is he?

"That's a good question. I think he's part terrier."

"There's definitely some beagle in him."

"Probably. Maybe some basset or suburban fence climber. All I know is he's one hundred percent lovable."

On cue, the mutt scrambled into a sitting position, whimpering, and smudged the passenger window with his nose.

Mental note to self: clean the bookmobile windows and deodorize the vehicle when they returned. "Yeah, to you. You'd take home a Tasmanian devil and pronounce it adorable."

Blue's brow furrowed and her lips pursed for a few seconds. "They do have sort of cute faces until they open their mouths, exposing all those sharp teeth. Rather like possums."

"You made my point. I want to try out the navigation system. Can you program Rivertown into it? I count myself lucky to snag a bookmobile with a navigation unit. This will make my life so much easier since I'm a little geographically challenged."

"A little?" Blue giggled. "Remember that time we were going to the big movie complex and you overshot it by thirty miles?"

"Ha! Yes, I remember." She grimaced as she recalled the incident. "Keep in mind, I just got my license and I'd never driven there on my own. Those exits are easy to miss when you're talking and blasting music at the same time."

"I'll give you that. Wait a minute. Let me put Moo down." She eased the now quiet dog to the floor, which he took as an opportunity to explore at foot level. When they fitted the vehicle with shelves, they tore out the damaged wall between the cab and van. Getting parts for older vehicles was about as easy as finding vintage collectibles at reasonable prices. Dallas had located what was needed in another state, which would mean another road trip. As for now, a ruffled curtain served as a partial barrier. Since it started at the floor to about a meter high, it turned out to be no barrier to the dog.

Slowing a bit, Tenny cast an anxious glance to the back of the van. "Is Moolah house trained?"

"Hard to say." Blue focused on typing in the address. "I've barely had him twenty-four hours. Oh sugar!"

"What? What's wrong?" Even though whatever vexed her friend had to do with the navigation system, Tenny still asked, "Is it the dog? Did he do something?"

"No, it's the navigation. It won't let me put in the address. Says it is a safety hazard in a moving vehicle. We'll have to stop."

"Ok. Not too surprising since a person could veer off the road or drift into another lane while trying to spell out a street address." A wide spot the school bus normally used for turns worked as a shoulder. "Once you get the address in, you need to gather your dog before he—" The sound of liquid streaming into the new commercial carpeting stopped her in mid-sentence.

Blue twisted in her seat to see her beloved dog. "Oh my!" She unbuckled her seatbelt and squeezed into the back of the van, knocking down the curtain partition in the process. "Do you have a towel?"

"I didn't think I'd need one." Nor did she think she'd have a dog peeing in her bookmobile on its first outing.

"No worries," Blue assured. She slipped the curtain off the spring pole. "I'll improvise."

"The smell." Tenny pointed out and noticed the tightness in her own voice.

"No problem," Blue's cheery voice announced. "I have some of the air freshener we use at the dairy in my purse. Throw it back here."

The bag landed with a splat, scattering a few items as it did so. "Sorry. Guess I should have zipped it up."

"That's all right." Blue's optimistic manner almost never faltered. It caused more than a few mean girls during high school to mock her without any real effect.

A few seconds later, a pungent citrusy smell stung Tenny's nose. "Geesh. It's that industrial orange smell. We'll have to drive with the windows down."

Blue squeezed back into the front with the dog tucked under her arm. She plopped down into her seat, and then read the message on the navigation screen. "This address can't be found."

"It's a sign," Tenny declared, hoping that would end their trip.

"We *have* to go. We've come this far."

Even though Tenny used logic whenever possible, she still felt like the big meanie pointing out the obvious. "We haven't even left town."

Certain that logic would rule the day, Tenny pulled at the steering wheel, easing into a U-turn that would bring them back into town where Blue could pick up her truck. Unfortunately, a hand latched onto her arm.

"What are you doing? I never took you for a quitter. The Tenny I know would be the first to embrace adventure. Besides, I have a general idea of how to get there. I've been there a number of times. I'll have to admit it's been more than a couple of years."

A question, a challenge, and one blatant lie. No one had ever used the word *adventure* in conjunction with Tenny's name. Maybe cautious, careful, even controlled, but never adventurous because

Tenny thought things out, trying to avoid the wrong thing even when she didn't know what it was. If Emerson possessed a therapist, they would have a field day with her, probably concluding her failure to be impulsive came from her mother's abandonment, which resulted in her need to be in control. They wouldn't be far off. It's weird to have a mother one day and then have her drive away without even saying goodbye. Single digits summed up her inner circle. Even though she had a feeling she'd regret it, she couldn't disappoint Blue.

"What else can happen?" Tenny pulled into a nearby driveway, reversed, and headed in the previous direction.

Chapter Four

AFTER ABOUT TEN miles of Moolah alternately barking at cars, cows, corn fields, and the occasional falling leaf, Tenny mentally sympathized with Griffin and his frustration with the ill-behaved addition to their family. Nothing calmed the pooch either. Turn on the radio and he howled—although Blue called it singing. Certain a rest stop might be needed, Tenny slowed as they entered a picturesque town with golden- and crimson-leaved trees lining the street. Wrought iron tables and chairs waited in front of a café, which was bordered by a bookstore and an antique shop. A few shoppers loaded down with bags conversed on the sidewalk. A sigh escaped Tenny. "A town of readers. It's kind of what I hope Emerson could be."

"Still can. It's not like it's ceased to exist. Like Rivertown," Blue pointed out. "Maybe we should stop. It's been a good thirty minutes. I'm sure Moolah could use a walk."

"That's the plan." Tenny spotted several empty spots near an Amish furniture and cabinet shop and parked the van. "I'm grateful that not too many people are buying cabinets today. It makes parking much easier. We can stop at the café and take turns going in, getting drinks, and using the restroom."

"Sounds like a plan." Blue waited until the engine switched off before she wiggled out of her seat while clutching the dog. Once on the sidewalk, she pulled a leash out of her purse and clipped it on.

Tenny observed the dog lunging at the end of the leash before she exited. Despite the charm of the town, she still locked the van which represented not only her current occupation but her aunt's dreams, too. Strangers waved at them. One older gentleman sporting overalls, a red checked shirt, and a green John Deere hat perched on his head strode closer and reached down to pat a straining-at-the-leash Sir Moolah, who responded by enthusiastically jumping on the dog lover. "Ya know, that dog would benefit from Marvin's Canine Stampede."

"What's that?" Blue asked with a smile while Tenny wondered about the use of *canine* and *stampede* together.

The man's eyes lit up as he explained. "It's a top-of-the-line doggy daycare and boarding kennel. Brand new. It has over ten fenced acres for your dog to romp with his own kind. Guaranteed to make your dog happy and tired. You should give it a go. I heard Marvin lets you have the first visit free to see if it suits your pal."

"Oh, no—" Blue remarked, probably ready to point out they weren't from around there.

Before she could, Tenny interrupted. "That sounds great! Where might we find this place?"

"It's off County Road 700 West as you head out of town." He winked, and spotting some other pedestrians, he hurried off to greet them. Even from a distance, they could hear his spiel about Marvin's Canine Stampede.

Blue chuckled and tugged on the leash to get the dog moving without success. Smells abounded near the ground and apparently, Sir Moolah needed to catalog each one. "He must be a one-man marketing team."

"Probably just a good friend." Noticing her friend's struggle with her pet, she realized it wouldn't be easy to gossip with the Rivertown locals while wrestling with a determined pooch. "We can drop off Moo at the dog place, then head to Rivertown, and pick him up on the way back."

"I don't know," Blue protested, giving another tug on the leash without any luck moving the dog away from a dropped candy wrapper. "He's rather delicate."

"Delicate?" She scoffed at the term. "This is a dog who lived on the streets. Why don't we go by the Stampede and check it out? If you like it, we can leave him. Who knows? Tracking down your cousin or the real thief might require more than one trip. It's hard to conduct a casual conversation while struggling with a wayward pup."

"He'll get better."

"Perhaps." Tenny hesitated to say more since she still shared quarters with a wily raccoon. "Not today, though. If we want to go into any buildings, we won't be able to do so with a dog—especially one who isn't housebroken. People tend to get testy about having their brand-new carpet initiated by a dog."

"Don't I know it." Blue fiddled with the dog leash, her hair swinging forward, hiding her face.

The statement surprised Tenny because she thought she hid her irritation reasonably well. Before Tenny could respond, Moo took advantage of an inattentive Blue, who'd loosened her grip on the leash, and jerked it out of her hand. He raced down the street after a fast disappearing black and white kitty. Both women, shocked at his action, stared open-mouthed until Blue lunged after the cat. "Moo!

Moo, come here!"

The canine darted in front of a car, resulting in honking and possibly a few choice words on the driver's part, but Moo managed to get to the other side of the street safely. A red-faced Blue pressed a hand to her heart as Tenny loped up beside her in time to hear her friend's gasped words. "Oh my! What kind of dog owner am I? I've barely had my dog a day, and he's gone."

"Not gone. He's just testing his limits. We'll find him." They hurried across the street, checking under cars, around trash cans, and near the butcher shop. No wayward hound to be found. Exhausted, the two of them plopped down on a convenient bench. Afraid her friend might cry, Tenny scoured her memory for one of those time-honored platitudes her aunt usually spouted, but couldn't remember any about runaway dogs.

A whistle caught her attention as the doggy daycare promoter headed their way, clutching Moo's leash, and the traitor dog walking nicely beside the man. Tenny nudged Blue, who cradled her head in her hands. "Look at that!"

Blue slowly lifted her head, blinked, and then spoke in almost a whisper. "It's Moo."

"And he's behaving!"

"True."

The man reached their bench and offered the leash with a flourish. "I believe I have something that belongs to you."

"Bless you." Blue reached for the leash. "How can I ever thank you?"

The man crinkled his nose. "No thanks are needed." He angled his head in the dog's direction. "Your little buddy might benefit from some training, though."

Even before he said the words, Tenny sensed them. The man didn't disappoint.

"You could get your pup trained at Marvin's Canine Stampede. That way, instead of running yourself ragged, all you'd have to do is whistle or tell him to come and he would."

Blue glanced down at Moo, then back to the man. "It sounds like a dream. Could Marvin teach him not to bark all the time, too?"

"That he can."

"My husband would like that very much." She turned toward Tenny. "What do you think?"

"Well," she hesitated, deciding to play a hunch. Putting up her index finger, she asked, "Are you Marvin?"

The man chuckled. "Guilty. You found me out." He pulled off his hat and used his free hand to rub his bald head. "I *do* have a state-of-the-art facility. It's kind of my field of dreams. I felt like when I finished building it, dogs would come. So far, no." His shoulders went up into a shrug. "Gives me plenty of time to drum up business. So, how about it?"

Blue grinned. "A visit sounds perfect. Since it happens to be a slow day for you, I'm willing to pay for some training."

"Housebreaking?" Tenny suggested, not anxious for another accident.

"You're a dreamer," Marvin added, clearly amused. "That would take a while longer. Give me a few hours and you'll be amazed."

They agreed to follow Marvin to his business after they grabbed a couple of drinks. About a mile or so out of town rested a crisp-looking facility with galvanized chain link fence surrounding the property. Several cute cut-outs of different dog breeds decorated the fence. If you squinted a little, it did look just the tiniest bit like they

M K SCOTT

were stampeding. They parked, exited, and headed for the front door.

Oversized windows let in the sunlight. On a whiteboard, someone, probably Marvin, had written *Make It A Barking Good Day.* Cute.

Before they could leave, Marvin insisted on showing them the interior, including the boarding area with automatic watering fountains and speakers mounted in each unit. "I usually play classical music. Arnie, my dog, prefers Hank Williams, but most like the long-haired stuff like Mozart."

The tour satisfied Blue enough that they waved goodbye to a happy Moo with Marvin, and climbed back into the bookmobile. Blue pulled her door shut. "Do you think I made a mistake leaving my baby here?"

"Nope. I think it would be a mistake bringing him along, and then trying to find out anything about your cousin. We'd be remembered as those annoying women with the disobedient dog."

"Maybe." She pursed her lips. "Why should we trust Marvin?"

Good question. "If he was up to no good, why spend all that money on building such a palace for dogs? He needs some word-of-mouth customers. *We* could be it. This is his dream."

"Yeah, you're right." Blue agreed, buckled up, and relaxed into her seat. "You have a way of explaining things that makes sense."

Pleased at the comment, Tenny silently added *it only works when people are ready to listen. So often, they aren't.*

24

Chapter Five

DROPPING SIR MOOLAH off at the Canine Stampede should have taken no time at all, but since Marvin wanted to show off his spanking new facility, they did the tour—a first-class place that possibly no one had ever heard of, or maybe it was just in the wrong location. Back when Tenny worked at the university library, almost all the staff had a dog, sometimes two, and usually kennels and doggie daycare served as lunch topics. Any one of her former co-workers would have jumped at such a nice place.

Dark clouds gathered, blocking the sun as Tenny pulled her door closed as the first raindrop hit.

"Timed that right." Her nose crinkled as she contemplated the joys of driving somewhere you didn't know in the rain. There were none. "Blue, you remember how to get there, right? It's probably been more than a few years since your last reunion. There's been quite a few road changes in the last six years—closures due to road construction, and that big limestone quarry. When I drove back to help Aunt Cinnamon, I was shocked at all the missing landmarks that let me know I was going the right way."

Her companion's blue eyes twinkled with a gleam of mischief as she answered. "Sure. It's Rivertown. Just head for the river. That has to still be there."

"Which river might that be?" Tenny asked well aware her friend occasionally joked on her.

Blue giggled, pointing to the road that ran in front of the Canine Stampede. "Get back on the road and head south. It isn't too far away. With any luck, the rain will have ended when we arrive."

As if it heard Blue's pronouncement and disliked it, the raindrops multiplied in speed and size, creating a deafening din. Only the lit console reassured Tenny that the engine turned over. Slow and steady wins the race, or at least that's what her uncle always said when teaching her how to drive. He also told her to check her mirrors whenever she got into the car. After checking all her mirrors, she turned on the defroster, certain she'd need it before long. It was better she'd do it now. Besides, if they kept talking, the windows would fog up in no time.

"Kitty litter in a sock does the trick."

Had she zoned out? "Uh, Blue, what are you talking about?"

"Get an old sock and fill it halfway with kitty litter. Make sure to tie it off tightly. I rubber band it to be sure and it cleans up your fogged windows just like that." She snapped her fingers for emphasis.

"I prefer the defroster method. Might as well see if it works."

"A traditionalist. It figures." She crinkled her nose. "Still, the kitty litter sock works if you're in a hurry."

Knowing her friend, a filled sock for defrosting purposes would eventually show up on her doorstep or passenger seat. "I'm thankful we found a place for your pup, but I'm surprised you agreed to the trial visit."

"Me, too." Blue audibly exhaled before continuing. "It was amazing how he got Moo to behave. He reminded me of my grandfather."

"How so?" Tenny eased onto the empty road. "Does your granddad like dogs? Is he bald? Or does he wear overalls all the time?"

"Grandpa Elliot hated dogs. He was an investment banker with a full head of silver hair. He almost always wore a suit. Casual meant a button-down shirt and khakis. I never saw him in a T-shirt."

"Okay." She bumped up the wiper speed and got a loud squeak. Should they sound like that? When she eyeballed the van initially, all she did was drive it around the block despite Dallas' urging her to try everything out before committing. Compared to the overpriced, questionable vehicles she'd already viewed, it earned the winner title. Another loud squeak sounded as the blade smeared water across the glass, doing little to clear it.

Her knuckles whitened as she gripped the steering wheel. As a glasses wearer, vision could be an issue. Her fingers went to her nose, feeling the plastic frames. Glasses on, but visibility almost none. She inhaled deeply and eased up on the gas pedal. Trying to distract herself from the inevitable, she asked, "So, how is Marvin like your Grandpa Elliot?"

The wiper blade on the driver's side moved a little slower, leaving behind good sized rubber chunks until only metal scratched the windshield. Wiper blades disintegrating the first time she used them. She snorted in disgust, remembering her intentions to change out the blades and then promptly forgetting to do so. The weather app made no mention of rain either. Tenny shut off the wipers, hoping to save the glass. She pulled over to the shoulder of the road, wishing she could go back to the moment when she had considered calling the whole trip off. They hadn't gone very far from the kennel, but in this rain, it might as well be a mile.

"Pipe tobacco. Almond cherry, I think." Blue's comment punctured the heavy silence.

"Excuse me?"

Blue cleared her throat and pointed at Tenny. "You asked me why Marvin reminded me of my grandpa Elliot. They both have that pipe smoke smell. My grandpa only smoked a certain brand. Despite smoking being bad for you and all that, when he smoked his pipe, he reminded me of Santa Claus."

Ernest Hemingway and Mark Twain both smoked pipes. Leave it to Blue to come up with a fictional character. "Sure. Did he have a red suit, a bowl full of jelly belly, or a tendency to say ho, ho, ho?"

She gave an emphatic head swing. "Nope. It was the pipe. As a kid, I didn't know anyone outside of Grandpa who smoked a pipe, so I put the two of them together. Probably warmed up to him a little more because of this—he wasn't your standard friendly grandpa with hard butterscotch candy in his pocket. I may have tried to make him nicer than he was. Anyhow, Marvin smells the same. I remember Grandpa Elliot going on and on about his pipe tobacco being imported. It wasn't cheap—even by his standards." She shrugged. "Didn't you smell it?"

"Possibly." She reached under her seat and pulled out a long bag. "I didn't have any context to attach the smell to. I guess your grandfather and Marvin both enjoy smoking pipes." She shook out long rectangular boxes from the bag.

"What's that?"

"Oh, that." Tenny grimaced, then sighed. "Windshield wipers. The thing Dallas warned me to replace immediately. I meant to. I even bought the blades but forgot to install them."

"Have you ever replaced your own wiper blades?" Blue asked

with raised brows.

"No, have you?" An uneasy feeling crept up her neck and hung out by her hairline, making her itch. "How hard can it be?"

"I guess you're about to find out. As for knowing how," she gave a derisive snort, "a big nope. As the only girl in the family, I was pampered, and then Griffin took over vehicle maintenance where my father left off."

"C'mon, I find that hard to believe. You can drive a tractor and help run a dairy, but you can't change a wiper blade?"

"No need to when someone else is willing to do it for me. Since this is your bookmobile, I imagine the maintenance falls on you."

"Yeah, yeah," Tenny grumbled, clutching the wipers, opening the door, and stepping out into a mud puddle and the rain. Before she even reached for the wiper arm holding what was left of the previous wiper, her cold, soaked clothes clung to her skin, making her shiver and grumble, "This day *has* to get better. It can't get any worse."

Chapter Six

THE RAIN STOPPED, giving way to gray skies and hovering clouds, which created a gloomy introduction to Rivertown. The colorful van should have made the residents smile, or at least be curious—if there *were* any residents. Only a caution light welcomed or possibly warned them with its continual blinking. Tenny slowed down in case another vehicle zoomed out of nowhere. An empty aluminum soda can tumbled across the street, pushed by the wind. On either side of the street were boarded-up storefronts. Signage still remained, such as Bertha's Beauty Hut and Roy's Smokes to Go. Closed drapes and a yellowed printed *Moved* sign told the story on one door. The oversized glass window on the other displayed the absence of customers, merchandise, and even a counter.

A heaviness filled the van. Most people never witnessed a death of a town. Places took on the emotions of their inhabitants. Thriving towns like Greenville they stopped in for a break earlier possessed a lively energy. If it could walk it would have a spring in its steps. Rivertown *shuffled*—and barely that. Tenny cut her eyes to Blue and asked, "Is anyone still here?" Before her friend could answer, she tacked on, "How did they relocate if the money vanished?"

Pointing to their surroundings, Blue replied in a solemn voice, unlike her usual cheerful tone, "This *was* the business section." She gave her head a slow shake. "It's been at least three or four years since I've been here. Usually, Jess always wanted to meet somewhere else." Her shoulders went up into a shrug. "Who could blame her? The last family get-together we had was a two hour's drive over in Parke County. You know, where all those covered bridges are? They rent shelters out there and my aunt snagged one. Anyhow," she paused, glancing outside, then continued, "I had no clue how bad it had gotten. Jess mentioned people moving out and shuttering their businesses. It's hard to survive without folks visiting your shop."

"So, most of these probably closed before the town decided to move?"

Blue shrugged. "Hard to know. Take a left at the next intersection. We might as well head out to my aunt's house since it looks like striking up casual conversation with the townspeople won't happen."

The illuminated red and blue Mobil gas station sign on the right caught Tenny's attention. Inside the minuscule mini-mart an employee could be seen. They might as well pull in since her uncle Mark used to tell her to get gas when you can because when you really need it, no station will be around. "I think I'll pull in here."

"Good choice," Blue agreed. "They used to pump your gas and even clean your windshield."

"Amazing. I'll have to see that."

Determined to conquer her first bookmobile fill-up at the gas station, she sucked in her lips and cautiously bumped into the parking lot. No other customers blocked the pumps, which pleased her as she eased in close enough to check the prices and moaned. "Good grief! They might as well ask for your firstborn."

"It's not like you *have* a firstborn. Besides, it's an opportunity to gossip. I'll go in while you pump gas." Blue suited her words to her actions.

No one hurried out to assist her with gas pumping or the wind-shield. Not too surprisingly, old-fashioned customer service no longer existed in Rivertown. Her initial attempt to pull the pump hose toward her vehicle met with resistance since Tenny miscalcu-lated where the gas tank intake was. At least the former owner filled up the tank before she sold it. With a huff, she climbed back into the van and moved it a foot, scampered out and repeated the whole process again, only to jump out of her shoes when a speaker mounted on the pole between pumps bleated.

"You need to pay first, then pump!"

"Okay!" Tenny called out, searched the pump for a credit card reader, and found none. She opened the van door and snagged her purse, muttering, "Whatever happened to people trusting you in small towns?"

Tenny strode to the mini-mart and opened the door, releasing the smell of burnt microwave popcorn along with a country music lyric about being done wrong. Already inside, Blue leaned against the counter with a fountain drink in hand as she chatted with a middle-aged man with a receding hairline and expanding waistline. A snippet of Blue's conversation carried. "That's too bad. What are you going to do?"

The man held out his hands and shrugged. "Isn't a whole lot I can do. Without money, I can't relocate. In a few months, Mobil will come and get their equipment. I'll be stuck in a town without a business."

Casual conversation served as her friend's strong point, not hers. The shelves contained a little bit of everything from diapers to dog

FROGS, FLOODS AND FRAUD

food, with an emphasis on *little*. Just a few packages of each item populated the shelves. It could be this was the last place Rivertown residents could pick up the essentials without driving on to the next town.

Inquisitive, she picked up a loaf of bread and turned it over to check the price. Seven dollars and sixty-nine cents! Her eyebrows shot up. It wasn't even one of those gourmet artisan loaves either. A slight squeeze with very little give demonstrated the white bread's staleness, which made her wonder how long it had sat on the shelf. Feeling bad for the shop owner, Tenny decided to buy something besides gas. She gently put back the bread and picked up a lunch bag size of popcorn.

The conversation stopped as she placed her treat on the counter. "I'd like ten dollars' worth of gas." She hesitated and reconsidered the amount with the price of gas and the van's hearty appetite. "Make that twenty dollars, plus the popcorn."

The man nodded, pressed a few keys on his register, and announced, "That will be twenty-four dollars and twenty-eight cents."

What started out as a simple trip kept getting more and more expensive. Tenny withdrew a couple of bills and handed them over. "Much business today?"

As he handed back her change, he said in a monotone voice, "You are my first customers and I count myself lucky for that. You must not be from around here." He angled his head in Blue's direction. "Her, I understand. She's on the way to see her aunt. What's your story?"

Asking a person why they were there or where they were headed might raise some red flags. Depending on the person, they might assume scam or serial killer. Crime and killers made occasional pit stops in small towns, but usually few and far between, which just left nosy residents well aware of outsiders.

Tenny pointed at Blue. "I'm her ride."

"Makes sense." He pressed his lips together as if contemplating the matter, and then added, "Make sure you girls take care."

Blue paid for her drink while Tenny turned over the man's statement. In a town as dead as Rivertown, should there be something they should worry about? Some unspoken danger? Perhaps he knew more than he was letting on. Never great with small talk, Tenny cleared her throat. "Is there anything we should be on the lookout for?"

The man reached up and scratched his ear, grimaced, and spoke. "Hard to say. Frogs are taking up residence everywhere. Coyotes are moving in closer. There's an unsettled feeling." He ran a hand over his five o'clock shadow and added, "Things aren't right. Like I said, you take care."

The two of them promised they would and left the store. Blue leaned against the van and sipped her drink as Tenny fueled the van. A gleaming sportscar pulled up on the other side of the pump. New car smell practically wafted off it as a dark-haired man, near Tenny's age, boosted himself out of the vehicle, nodded in their direction, and said, "Afternoon, ladies." They both mumbled a reply. Surprised at the second customer, both Blue and Tenny's gaze followed his swagger until he disappeared inside the mini-mart.

"Not local," Blue said, taking another pull on her drink.

"You know everyone?" Tenny arched one eyebrow as she held onto to the gas pump nozzle. Even though her bestie had relatives in town, she doubted her ability to catalog every resident.

"Nah." She cocked her head in the direction of the store. "Oh, he's a townie playing at country. His jeans are new, his boots unscuffed, and no one I know would wear a jacket like that."

Her brows furrowed as she tried to remember the jacket. All she could pull up was dark. "No one wears dark jackets around here?"

"It was a fashion jacket. Something high end that has to be dry cleaned. Not something you'd feed livestock in or wear inside your combine."

"Never knew you were a fashion expert."

"Just practical work clothes." She dusted the fingernails of her free hand on her shirt. "He might work for you, though. I didn't notice a ring."

"Not interested. My taste runs to men with light-colored hair."

"Yeah, I noticed." Blue sidled over to the car.

"Blue!" Tenny hissed. "What are you doing?"

"Getting info. Lots of people would like to know about a handsome fellow passing through town. Gossip is like a currency. You have to have some to get more." She blew out a breath in disgust. "Nothing. Car's spotless. Either he hasn't had it long or it's not his."

The gas pump clicked off and Tenny nudged her friend. "You done gawking?"

"For now."

Initially, Tenny thought to ask Blue if she'd pried a nugget of information from the station owner, but an upward glance at the speaker stopped her. She assumed he could eavesdrop on them. Hopefully, the new customer kept him busy, or they both could have listened to their busybody conversation. In that case, they needed to be long gone before a major awkward moment occurred with the man's returning. Blue parted her lips as if to speak. Tenny lifted her brows and angled her head toward the speaker.

Whatever Blue might have said changed to, "You hungry? It's past lunchtime."

"I'm okay." Her stomach growled, disproving her words. "Besides, I have popcorn."

"Uh-huh." Blue acknowledged.

After putting up the nozzle, Tenny wrinkled her nose at the sharp sting of gasoline, which reassured her as she tightened the cap. With things being as bad as they were, it wouldn't be too surprising if the shop owner watered his gas. Then again, his customers would most likely be his neighbors and relatives.

Once inside the van, Blue practically quivered waiting for Tenny to shut the driver's side door. The engine started with a low hum and she shifted into drive, moving slowly past the pumps. Blue waved, certain the store owner would be watching. He was.

"Guess what?" Blue chirped.

Sometimes getting information from her bestie often became a game of twenty questions. "What did you find out?"

"Larry thinks Jess didn't take the money!"

"Who's Larry?"

"The gas station owner." Blue said the words matter-of-factly, as if everyone knew that.

"All right, he told you Jess didn't do it. Did he perhaps tell you who did? Any suspects?"

Blue exhaled audibly, then sniffed. "Nope. He may have been the last person to see Jess, though."

"How so?" It would be nice to have an easy answer to everything. Then she could go home and work on her schedule for her mobile library community visitation.

"She filled up her tank before leaving town." Blue's enthusiasm dimmed a little as she slumped back into her seat. "It's not anything, really. Said she was in a hurry and paid with wadded dollar bills and a bunch of quarters. That doesn't sound like someone with tons of money."

"True." Tenny searched her mind for questions that one of Aunt Cinnamon's favorite television detectives might ask. "Was anyone else with her?"

"Don't know. I didn't ask and Larry didn't say. Besides, she paid with loose change. If I had someone with me, I'd make them pay their fair share of gas money, especially at Larry's."

"Depends. If she wanted to throw suspicions elsewhere, paying in change might do it." She turned left at the next intersection, passing houses with dead flowers in their flower boxes. With fall's approach, dead flowers weren't an oddity. However, many would have cut the dead flowers and replaced them with colorful mums, or even artificial flowers to enliven their yards. Not here, though, when people expected not to be around much longer. She mulled over Jess' voluntary exit—it shouted *guilty* big time. "We know Jess is still around or was recently. That's a plus."

"You're right. We just have to find her." Blue's chipper tone returned. "We should have this wrapped up by the weekend."

Chapter Seven

THE CRACKED ROAD crumbling at the edges eroded even more as the houses grew farther and farther apart. Clouds stacked on top of one another as if crowding in for a Black Friday sale. The industrial citrus deodorizer still overwhelmed a bit, forcing Tenny to crack her window while not drawing Blue's attention. Possibly having a felonious cousin and trying to help said cousin occupied her friend's thoughts—no need to remind her of her less-than-perfect pooch. The road ahead became a series of holes held together by very little pavement, causing her to cut her already modest speed. "It looks like Swiss cheese as opposed to a lane. The water inside the holes worries me. I had a coworker who lost a rim in a water-filled pothole. There's no telling how deep they are."

Blue leaned forward in her seat and stared out the windscreen. "Never a great road..." She gave a dismissive sniff and then continued. "...but this is ridiculous! Maybe driving on the shoulder would be better. It's not that far to Aunt Hazel's house. I'm sure she'll offer us lunch." She twisted in her seat to address Tenny. "It's important you accept anything she offers you. She's very sensitive about her cooking."

That sounded ominous. Still watching the road, Tenny muttered her agreement as her eyes passed over the gravel-dusted shoulder. It wasn't overly wide. Too far and she'd tip into a ditch from which no AAA motor service could rescue her. Her membership might not honor campers heavy with books. She'd check into that once they got back home. She grimaced as she imagined the hole-pocked road resembling a game of whack-a-mole. Maybe it would be more like the childhood game they played, which they named Escape from Burning Lava Island where they jumped from couch to chairs, pretending the hardwood floor transformed into a molten, smoldering mass. As she recalled, her aunt wasn't a fan of the game, but her uncle remarked on their imaginations. It would take more than imagination to get across this road. Knowing she'd probably regret it, she turned on her fog lights, as if that would help, and steered toward the shoulder.

The bookmobile wobbled as a back tire caught on a deep hole, but thankfully the other three touched the shoulder and pulled the tire free. There was a bit of a jolt and page fluttering, indicating a few books had flopped to the floor in the effort. Keeping one eye on the side mirror, she straightened the vehicle so it stayed between the ditch and the road. Just looking at it made her uneasy. Trypophobia brought on fear, disgust, or even nausea when presented with holes of some kind. She knew this because a psychology student needed help with her term paper on phobias. Yes, those gaping holes filled with murky water did bring on anxiety, but possibly because they could destroy the undercarriage of her bookmobile.

"Not much farther," Blue encouraged. Never mind they had barely moved ten feet.

A lightning charge illuminated the interior with harsh light, forcing her to slam on the brakes and squeeze her eyes shut against the glare. A menacing crashing sound pried open her eyes as a sizable maple tree toppled onto the road and a thunderclap erupted so close it rattled the vehicle.

A gasp sounded in the cab. Unsure if she or Blue had made the sound, Tenny cleared her throat. Good thing they weren't actually using the road.

"Okay, now." Tenny pushed out the words through gritted teeth. Her very inconvenient memory chose that moment to remind her that her public speaking professor marked her down for saying *okay* too much. He called it a stalling mechanism. Stalling, my foot. It was a coping mechanism, which helped when she had no clue as to what to say. "Looks like more rain. It's hard to say how long it will be before this road is impassable—although I'd probably say it already was."

"Um…" Blue stammered stopping as a water deluge emptied over the van. Perhaps she said something else but it was impossible to hear.

The headlights showed a patch of the road about five feet ahead, which resulted in driving a little under ten miles an hour. A metal sign popped out of nowhere and smacked the side of the van, resulting in a metallic screech.

Startled, Tenny yelped. "Son of a gun! What was that?"

"Bridge sign!" Blue shouted the words to be heard over the rain.

The word *bridge* had her slamming the brakes again. "There's a bridge up ahead?"

"Yes!" Blue nodded, emphasizing her point.

That meant the road, what existed of it, connected to the bridge while the shoulder would only lead to water and a disagreeable ending to an already bad day. "Geesh. That means we'll have to use the road."

If Blue heard, she gave no indication, no word of advice. Only the rain interspersed with the growl of thunder could be heard with the unwelcome illumination of nearby lightning. Sitting here on the side of the road, they were probably little more than a mobile lightning rod. Most people liked to think rubber tires grounded them, but vehicles with windows opened were often victims. Tenny peeled her whitened fingers from the steering wheel and closed the cracked window she'd opened due to the pungent deodorizer, slick with invading raindrops. She blew out a heavy breath as she stared at the rain-soaked surroundings. The pounding slowed to a steady patter, indicating a possible break in the storm. No help for it—she couldn't go back, she had to go forward.

Pushing her shoulders back, she eased the vehicle very slowly onto the road. A shudder, then a dip, followed by a lurch, then a clatter of more falling books, caused Tenny to wince. *Keep going,* she mentally encouraged herself. The sight of the green metal bridge visible up ahead motivated her. All she had to do was make it to the bridge and cross over. After a painful twenty feet, the van tires touched the bridge and Tenny released her breath.

Easy sailing. Halfway across the bridge, Blue glanced outside and then *harrumphed* to herself, muttering something indecipherable.

"What?"

"My aunt won't even drive across the bridge; afraid it might bust under the weight of her Ranger truck. Paranoid about the rust. Claims only the paint holds it together."

Familiar with the small size of the truck model, the bookmobile probably weighed twice as much—not a comforting thought in the middle of the bridge. Stepping on the gas on a wet bridge might invite disaster, too. Better yet, why was she even here? Oh yeah, friendship—why did she keep forgetting that?

"Um, your aunt, does she never leave the area because of the bridge?"

The rain slowed, making conversation at a slightly louder level than normal a possibility. "Oh, no. She just uses the other road. It connects with the state road. Avoids the bridge, the potholes, and the town altogether."

Even though she probably wouldn't like the answer, Tenny still inquired. "So, we could have gone down this other road and avoided all this?"

"Sure." Blue answered matter-of-factly. "But we would have missed talking to Larry and getting our excellent eyewitness testimony. Our point was to mingle with the locals to get the hot gossip."

"Takes locals to mingle." While her expectations never climbed higher than the residents coming out of their homes at the sight of unknown vehicle, even that modest goal died at the sight of the deserted business district. As for excellent eyewitness testimony? Oh yes, Larry and his observation that Jess only had dollars and change—which still could be important. Grudgingly, she admitted, "I guess you're right."

Her heartbeat steadied as they exited the bridge and could see a neat brick house in the distance. Blue gestured emphatically. "Look! We're here."

Chapter Eight

THE RAIN SLOWED to a few random drops, and a ray of sunlight broke through the clouds as Tenny pulled into the gravel driveway. Glad for a break from the road and its numerous perils, she placed the vehicle in park, switched off the ignition, and flopped back into the seat. Who knew driving a bookmobile could be as nerve-wracking as plunging down a roller coaster hill—over and over again? Unlike many roller coaster fans, she avoided deliberately shaking hands with danger if she could avoid it.

The screen door crashed open as a petite, middle-aged woman emerged in a leopard-spotted nylon pants and windbreaker. Only a wisp of bright red bangs peeked out from the turban. She smiled and waved with large expansive moves as if guiding in an aircraft for landing. Knowing the probable answer, Tenny still asked, "Your aunt?"

"Yep…" Blue answered as she unbuckled her seatbelt. "I called ahead this morning. She knew we were coming. We might as well go in or Aunt Hazel will rip open the doors and practically carry us in."

"Okay…" She stopped herself before she could finish, realizing the simple acknowledgment sometimes did serve as a stalling mechanism. "You go ahead. I want to pick up all the books that fell. The dry run may have flopped, but no reason for books to get damaged."

Blue slid from her seat, moved to where the woman waited, embraced her, and the two walked inside, but not before the aunt directed a curious glance toward Tenny. Visitors normally were red letter events in small towns. No doubt the woman had prepared a nice meal. The very least she could do was hurry up. No cook enjoyed serving up cold or overcooked food. With the many sumptuous meals Cinnamon made in mind, and expecting something similar, if not exactly in the same league, she squeezed through to the library portion. Her mouth watered at the thought of cornflake-dipped fried chicken, Salisbury steak, or chicken and dumplings. About a dozen books rested in disarray on the floor, with a few opened face down on the carpet. Tenny smoothed her hands over the pages as if wiping away the abuse. Once the fallen books were snug back into their places, she headed to the house.

Knocking once, Tenny waited for a *come in!* before doing so. No tantalizing aromas of savory or sweet treats welcomed her. Instead, the dry smell of paper, cardboard, and dust reigned. Blue's voice drew her to the kitchen where a large road map covered the table along with an open notebook with a few lines scribbled on its college-ruled pages. Where was the meal Blue promised? Feeding visitors served as a basic country hospitality, especially among the older generation. There was nothing on the counter either, unless she considered an almost empty coffee pot as lunch worthy. Blue and her aunt traded news about people Tenny didn't know. Her aunt dipped her head into an open cabinet and withdrew, brandishing a can. "Found it!"

"Oh good." Blue clapped her hands together, twisting at the waist to include Tenny in the conversation. "My aunt is going to make us beanie weenies."

Aunt Hazel announced with a grin, "It was always Blue's favorite meal."

"How nice," Tenny responded, but turned slightly to her friend, mouthing the question, "when?"

Blue's upheld five fingers served as an answer. Her earlier comment about appreciating whatever was served made sense considering the aunt might be a couple of decades behind when it came to her niece's favorite foods. The meal wouldn't be in Aunt Cinnamon's league. So far, no one had ever come close. Silence stretched as Hazel dumped beans into a pot and then searched for the elusive hot dogs in the freezer section of her fridge.

"What's with the map?" She meant the question more for Blue.

With her head stuck in the freezer, Hazel answered, her voice a little muffled. "Got to find somewhere to go with the town moving."

It was odd that she'd still be moving when Larry's opportunities came to a halt with the funds disappearing. Could be she was just entertaining herself with prospects, certain the money would return. "Found anything?"

"Smoked sausage," Hazel announced, pulling out a frozen rope of sausage. "Not wieners, but it could work."

"Sounds great," Blue chimed in.

Somehow, her friend was missing some vital information. If Hazel, Jess' mother, had money to relocate, it did nothing to argue against her daughter's being the thief. "I meant, where are you thinking of relocating?"

Instead of replying immediately, her brow furrowed as her eyes rolled upward. "Good question. Most of the townspeople wanted to move away from the flood zone, but not so far that they'd change their entire lives. A couple of miles away, they can still shop at the same stores, attend the same church, and visit their friends. Not me, though." She pursed her lips and placed the frozen sausage on the counter with a thud. "With Jess leaving, there's not much for me here. As you probably heard, everyone thinks my girl ran away with the money, being the treasurer and all."

Even though her suspicions were similar, Tenny chose not to mention them. Innocent until proven guilty, and all that. "Blue may have mentioned something to me."

"Not surprised." She patted Blue's shoulder in passing and then shoved the frozen sausage into the microwave to defrost. "Anyhow, I've considered a lot of places, and none of them close to my former traitorous friends." She sniffed dismissively, then continued. "There's Corydon—it's higher in elevation. Then, there's Craw-fordsville. Even though it's much bigger than here, I heard it still retains its small-town charm."

"True," Blue commented. Catching Tenny's raised eyebrows, she added, "Shouldn't you wait until Jess comes back?"

"I'm not sure she's coming back." Hazel leaned against the counter. "It's never been a secret her goal in life was to move somewhere else more exciting. When this town move came about, she was all for it. She even volunteered to be treasurer. Jess has some bookkeeping experience due to working at Roy's Smokes To Go."

It made her a decent candidate for treasurer. When it came to community money, usually two people had to sign the check, sometimes even three. The case against Jess was definitely stronger than the one for her being innocent of financial shenanigans. Still, why would someone volunteer and then steal the money, since she'd be the obvious suspect? In all the mystery novels and shows, the most obvious person was never guilty. Often, it turned out to be someone who appeared guiltless since they worked hard to create that image.

Tenny feigned coughing, not feeling comfortable questioning this woman, she didn't know. With any luck, Blue would know the right questions. Being related allowed a certain nosiness. With as long as it took to get here, not once had Blue popped the obvious question. Her hesitation was saying the wrong thing—such as Jess' having the opportunity to take the money and run, which would strain their friendship.

Without asking, Hazel filled up a glass of water and handed it to Tenny. After she guzzled the water, she leveled a penetrating look at her friend, who acted surprised and then said, "Jess left without saying anything?"

"Not to me, at least. I went down to the VFW in Fieldstown with Barbara Ann. They have Coverall Bingo on Tuesday nights and pizza rolls!"

Whoever came up with the names for surrounding towns needed another job, but as far as answering the question, Hazel hadn't. Keeping her hand close to her hip, she circled it a little, asking for Blue to get more details. Fortunately, the two of them had created gestures they both knew once Uncle Mark explained how coaches often use hand gestures to relay moves. The two of them adapted coaching moves for their own benefit, possibly confusing anyone who observed them.

Blue held up one finger. "Are you saying you never saw her before she left?"

"Nope, I never did."

That meant two people living in the same household casually

parted without exchanging a word. Even though Tenny's mother left her daughter without an explanation, she expected better from other folks. "Didn't you try to call her?"

"I did." The microwave buzzed, cutting into the conversation and drowning out the rest of the statement.

"What?"

"Did me no good." She pulled out the sausage, grabbed a steak knife, and peeled the plastic away before cutting the sausage into chunks and dropping it into the bean pot. "Turns out her phone was here all along."

"No way!" Blue straightened from her relaxed pose. "People her age have their phones on them all the time."

"I thought that, too." Hazel switched on the burner and picked up a wooden spoon for stirring. "Then again, she kept getting hateful calls with people calling her all sorts of evil names. Mainly her harassers texted since cell service is iffy. Makes me understand why she might not want it."

"I can see that," Blue concurred. "Still, it's hard imagining some-one her age without a phone."

"Oh." Hazel's shoulders went up into a shrug. "She could always get another one at the discount store. And buy some minutes, too."

"So," Blue started, angling her head in her aunt's direction, "did you get the new number?"

Her aunt stopped stirring long enough to shake her head. "Prob-ably better off not knowing." She inhaled deeply. "There are things going on in this town. Whispers here and there. Odd things. Might even say dangerous. Cars that no one recognizes going through town. Garcia's Angus cattle got out and they put up an extra heavy fence, too."

Tenny smirked as Blue rolled her eyes, knowing her friend was partial to dairy cows as opposed to beef cattle. Surely, she'd say something.

"Angus," Blue snorted. "They always try to escape. That's who they are."

"At night?" Aunt Hazel asked, possibly knowing her niece's bovine preferences.

"Well…" Blue hesitated, pursed her lips, and said, "No. Cows don't normally wander at night unless something frightens them like a mountain lion, snake, or any other type of predator."

"Strange doings." Hazel crossed her arms and shook her head slowly. "Leaving is the only thing I can do."

"How will Jess find you?" Blue hunched her shoulders, clearly disturbed by the possibility of her cousin's not being able to locate her mother.

"Oh, she's a smart girl." She glanced away and stirred the bubbling pot. "Besides, she knows my number. That much hasn't changed."

While buying a new phone could be a real possibility, there also existed the likelihood of a mother lying to protect her child. Blue inquired where Jess had gone while Tenny mentioned a need for the bathroom.

"Down the hall to your right. In a house this size, you can't miss it. I'm looking forward to a bigger house with more than one bathroom."

How would that happen with the funds missing? The conversation drifted from the kitchen with Blue asking where Jess might have gone and her aunt replying she could have joined the circus for all she knew. Goodness! Didn't the woman keep up with the times?

There were hardly any circuses left.

Half-filled boxes and light-colored rectangles on the wallpapers where pictures once hung told the moving tale. She headed to the bathroom, peering into a bedroom with a zebra-striped bedspread, which probably belonged to Hazel. A suitcase rested on top of the bed.

Bright splashes of yellow, spring green, and turquoise blue on the walls, spread, and curtains brightened the second bedroom. Carefully arranged black and white autographed photos of celebrities decorated one wall. Those pics must mean a lot to Jess, which would mean she'd pack them if she expected to be gone long.

On the bedside table was a torn scrap of paper with a phone number written on it. No name, just the number. Tenny pulled out her phone and captured it in a photo. Blue might recognize the number. Even though being caught in the room could raise a stink, she decided to play a hunch and pushed the sliding closet door open. Not easy to do, since so many clothes pushed on the other side of the door, making it hard to open. If Jess left, then she left in a hurry, taking almost nothing. *Why*? Was she afraid? Did someone threaten her? Why pack if you could just buy a better version of her previous possessions?

Chapter Nine

LARGE, MURKY PUDDLES dotted the road—in a few lower spots, the water covered the entire road. A half-submerged bullfrog gave Tenny a feel for how deep the water was as she guided the bookmobile cautiously through the water. Can't be that deep or the bullfrog wouldn't be visible. Then again, it could be a ginormous bullfrog or possibly resting on a rock.

Dark clouds scudded across the low, gray sky. The weather suited her current mood. The dry run her friend suggested should have been an easy drive, not some expedition across a flood-devastated land. She cleared her throat before addressing her fellow passenger and suggester of the dry run. "Ah, Blue. Did you say this was the good road?"

"Used to be," she replied casually, pointing ahead. "Look at the river. It's almost breaching its banks. Thank goodness Aunt Hazel is moving. It makes me wonder what fool bought her home."

"Me, too," Tenny added, narrowing her eyes as a stream rippled across the road. "Not sure how she could sell it if the government already gave her a payout."

"Money she never got."

"Not sure the government will see it that way." Making her best guess, Tenny firmed up her lips and steered to the left. The driver's side tire dropped for a heartbeat, then popped out of the hole it discovered under the water. Her held breath escaped with a whoosh of relief—only, it may have been too soon. A hard jerk caused several books to fall and something metallic clanged in the reading area. *Great.* The next time they stopped, she'd investigate. Right now, she needed to get to the next place. With this in mind, Tenny goosed the gas pedal—only to hear the engine whine without any forward motion. She eased off the gas, waited ten seconds, and tried again with the same results.

Before she could try for the third time, Blue said, "We're stuck. Might as well get out and check it. It's not like anyone will come by and help us."

"You're right," Tenny admitted before putting the vehicle into park and switching off the engine. Even though she wanted to complain about the latest disaster, she stifled the urge. She swung open the door and waited for Blue to do likewise. Outside, a robin vocalized, making the scene a little less grim.

The bookmobile cab was set a little higher than a regular sedan, so Tenny used the running board as a step. Not considering her environment, she hopped feet first into murky water, hitting the hidden slippery mud.

"Hey!" Tenny's hands flew up in the air, doing nothing to break her fall as her smooth-soled shoes failed her. Splash! The large frog she used to gauge the water depth croaked an alarm and leaped past her, drenching her with muddy water in the process. A good six inches of water soaked her bottom and feet. Blue rounded the front of the vehicle at a jog. "What's happened?"

When she witnessed Tenny sitting in the muddy water, she did what any close friend would do. She laughed. Despite Tenny's grimace, she laughed some more, and then offered her hand. Once upright, the two of them made their way to the back of the bookmobile where the driver's side back tire rested halfway in the water. The slight tilt of the vehicle told the story.

With so many other things she'd rather do than confirm her suspicions, Tenny squatted, grabbed the exposed portion of the tire for balance, and moved her hand underwater in an exploration effort. Not knowing what might reside in the water caused her to bite her bottom lip. Any reasonably intelligent critter would be long gone due to the bookmobile's splashing through the water. It would just be her luck to encounter a frightened water snake.

The research part of her brain listed the types of water snakes found in Indiana. Most of them had names that included the label *water snake*: Common Water Snake, Plain Belly Water Snake, Diamond-backed Water Snake. Her fingers were on the tread of the tire as Tenny recalled none of the mentioned snakes were poisonous. All the same, she'd prefer no snake bites, poisonous or otherwise. She slid her fingers deeper into the cool water, wincing as she did so. No one had ever accused her of being a tomboy growing up. As soon as she learned to read at the tender age of four, reading was her sport of choice. Talk about being out of her comfort zone.

Blue half squatted and peered at the tire. "Is it stuck?"

Something scuttled across Tenny's hand. She jerked it out of the water so fast that she plopped back into the water, and then scrambled upright with a gasp, pressing her dirty hand over her heart. "Oh no!"

"Oh no, what?" Blue furrowed her brow as she casually inquired.

Tenny lifted one foot high, then the other, as if in a very showy marching band or a demanding exercise class. "I just remembered one of Indiana's water snakes is the poisonous cottonmouth. When I had my hand in the water, something touched it!"

"It must have been a twig, an insect, or a crawdad," Blue offered as she straightened up. "Cottonmouths aren't all that common in Indiana."

"Common enough to be listed as an Indiana water snake, which means plenty of people have encountered them."

"Maybe so," Blue conceded. "Still, there's no cottonmouth down there. If there had been, it would have bitten you."

The high stepping marching slowed until Tenny stood still, staring downward. "Something *did* touch me."

"I believe you. What about the tire? Is it stuck?"

Not willing to put her hands back into the opaque water, Tenny resorted to Uncle Mark's logic model. The bookmobile couldn't go forward, there were tons of gaping potholes everywhere, and the vehicle tilted due to one tire being lower than the others. Some might call that circumstantial evidence, but it worked for her. "It's stuck."

"Well then." Blue placed both hands on her hips. "Looks like we're going to have to rock it out. You push. I'll drive."

Tenny watched her friend saunter toward the driver's door. Her lips pursed as she considered the joys of pushing a dirty bookmobile stuck in a watery pothole. "Wait! Why don't you push? You're bound to be stronger. Working with cows and all."

It made sense to her, but Blue giggled and called back. "I'm clean! You're not. It makes sense you would push. It *is* your bookmobile. Besides, I know how to do this since our farm vehicles get stuck all the time."

While her reasoning had merit, Tenny stuck her tongue out, wiped her hands on her shirt, and assumed her position behind the bookmobile.

Chapter Ten

THE CLOUDS PLAYED tag with a weak sun, often blotting out the meager light, making it feel later than it actually was. Instead of the glorious birdsong of before, everything went silent or maybe Tenny just couldn't hear anymore after being exposed to the loud whirl of the tire, the choking exhaust, and the mud splatter.

She glared at the problematic rear tire. Now out of the humongous pothole and sitting on the pavement with the other three tires, it no longer stalled their trip. Wet, muddy, and generally disgusted, Tenny stomped to the driver's door just as Blue exited and offered her a length of fabric. Tenny accepted the fabric and used it to wipe the mud clumps creating damp smears on her jeans and shirt. With the majority flaked off, people wouldn't mistake her for some river monster that snatched strolling couples from the shore. She searched for a clean spot of the fabric to wipe her face off. As she held it up, she sniffed, halted, and when she recognized the telltale scent of a dog, blurted out, "Blue!"

"Hey!" Her lips pulled up in an apologetic smile. "It was the only thing available for wiping the mud off."

"Yeah." She blew out a breath, barely ruffling her muck-flecked bangs. "Who knew I should have packed towels and a change of clothes? Maybe I should have thrown in some dry shampoo, too."

There was no reason to take it out on her friend. These things happen. Her shoulders went up into a shrug as she tried for a grin and failed. "At least we can head straight home and I won't run into anyone."

Blue cleared her throat. "Don't forget Sir Moolah."

"How can I, since I now smell like him, along with a few more unsavory scents."

Not answering, Blue circled the front of the vehicle and climbed into the passenger side. Tenny glanced at the clean seat and placed the empty plastic bag from the gas station mini-mart on it. It was not ideal as a seat guard, but it should work.

The passenger side door slammed as Tenny boosted herself in and started the engine, pulling her own door closed. Home, a bath, maybe cereal eaten in front of a television—it appealed. Now all she had to do was get from here to there.

"Ya know," Blue started in a wheedling tone, "a specialty coffee would improve your mood. Something with cinnamon and whipped cream."

"Outside of actually teleporting home, nothing will improve my mood. Besides, you're the one who likes all those fancy coffees. I'm willing to bet there's no Starbucks coffee shop nearby. My goal is to have no contact with other humans."

"What about the kennel?"

"Your dog." She pushed out the words and flicked the heater to high. "You go inside to get him. Surely you can handle him."

"You're right," Blue offered in a soft voice.

"Which way?"

"This road runs straight to the river, then you hang a left."

After shifting the vehicle into drive, Tenny sighed. "I'm not mad at you. It's pretty much everything that's happened today has really got my goat. Here we are leaving Rivertown without knowing much more than when we came."

"Oh…" Blue lengthened the word. "That's not true."

"Like what?" Tenny scanned the area for any gaping potholes ready to do battle with her bookmobile as she waited for her friend's reply.

"We know Jess wasn't heading out of town with money dripping out of her pockets if she was paying with change and dollar bills for gas."

That much she'd agree on. Tenny sniffed and gave her friend a quick glance, causing Blue to sit up straighter and demand, "What? I know that look. What did you do?"

No one would associate Tenny with any cloak-and-dagger stuff, which made it easy for her to engage in casual nibbing. "Ah, you know when I asked to go to the bathroom?"

"I knew it!" Blue gave an emphatic nod. "I was listening and didn't hear a toilet flush. Aunt Hazel's toilet groans and you have to jiggle the handle. No one can slip into the bathroom without everyone noticing."

"Oh!" Tenny scrunched up her nose. "You think she noticed?"

"I doubt it." Blue chuckled. "The woman was in full righteous indignation that people would consider her daughter a thief just because she disappeared the same time the money did."

"Funny that." Her uncle Mark used to say the simplest explanation was usually the right one. Sure, it never worked that way on a crime drama. "I *did* peek in the bedrooms."

"You find out anything?"

"Your aunt has a great love of animal prints."

"Growing up, I thought she'd been on safari and shot animals for their pelts. When I found out she picked them up at the local discount store, I was relieved." Blue gestured with her hand for Tenny to continue. "Anything else?"

Thinking about the suitcase on Hazel's bed, Tenny said, "It looks like your aunt is in a hurry to leave. Packing up everything not nailed down."

"I'd expect that with Jess gone." Blue played with a strand of hair, twisting it, and letting it go, only to repeat the action. "I'm just surprised Jess didn't text or anything. That's not like her."

"Well, I don't really know her, except what you told me over the years. I always thought she looked up to you."

"Me, too." Blue grimaced. "Not sure why. I was older than her and that's about it. I remember what it was like being young and people not taking you seriously so made a point to listen to her."

"Yeah, that would do it." The road widened a little, possibly for a bus turnaround, but Tenny kept to the middle as she conversed. "I did notice in her room she had all these framed, autographed celebrity photos."

"Oh, yeah." A smile flitted across Blue's face. "Jess loves her celebs. She's been writing fan letters forever. I helped her when she was younger with spelling. It surprised me she got so many replies. Then again, she goes after unusual folks such as scientists, not your popular movie stars, but someone in the background most people miss, and a handful of animal activists and environmentalists. Every time she opened up an envelope with a signed photo inside, it was like Christmas morning."

That answered one question. "So, you're saying she wouldn't leave without them?"

"No." She gave her head a slow shake. "I assume they're still in her room?"

"Yep," Tenny acknowledged. "Nicely arranged and hanging on the wall. Her closet is so packed I could barely get the door open. This isn't a gal who packed a bag or two. At first, I thought maybe she planned on buying a new wardrobe with her extra cash."

"Tenny!" Blue reached across the console and rapped her friend's arm. "You should be ashamed of yourself."

"One of us has to be practical." She held up her right hand as if to halt any potential rapping while keeping her left hand on the steering wheel. "The photos tell a different story. A person doesn't collect something for that long to just abandon it. Sure, she might meet a guy who might ridicule it and she might even hide it for a little bit. Once she sees the guy for what he is, it all goes back on the wall. This makes me wonder if Jess meant to leave that day."

Blue murmured something as she stared at her phone.

"What?"

"You wouldn't believe how many messages I have from construction companies on my phone. Griffin and I discussed extending the milking barn. I went online and tried to get an estimate for what it would cost." She blew out a breath. "All of a sudden, they want your email and phone number before they'll give you a quote. Calls at all times of the day and night. I blocked most of them. Now I get texts. Geesh, I can't even find texts from people I know." She grumbled a little more as she clicked and scrolled. "Oh my!"

"What? What is it?" Tenny braked lightly, then stopped, seeing no traffic either way. Her friend's alarmed tone worried her. "Griffin?"

As an answer, Blue held out her phone. A text message from Jess read: *Call me, Margo. I think I need advice.*

"Margo?"

"It's an inside joke."

That explained why she hadn't heard from her cousin. "You need to call her."

She pecked quickly at the phone. "Doing it now. Looks like she texted me the day she left town. Stupid contractors clogging up my feed. I will admit to ignoring texts since I thought it would be just more of the same."

Chapter Eleven

THE BOOKMOBILE IDLED in the middle of the empty rural road as Blue called back her cousin's number. A few scraggly pines loomed around them, almost leaning as if listening. A few raindrops hit the vehicle rooftop, echoing, resulting in Tenny asking, "Is it on speaker? I want to hear."

Blue pushed a button and the *brr-ring* of the phone filled the interior. After five rings, Tenny shrugged and wondered aloud, "No voicemail?"

"She definitely has it."

Then a click indicated pick up and a familiar voice said, "Hello?"

Success! Tenny's grin melted. She shouldn't recognize the voice of someone she'd never met. Her friend held the phone to her ear. "Ah, Aunt Hazel. I was trying to reach Jess."

Because the phone was still on speaker, Hazel's voice carried. "As we all are. This is her phone, but I did say she left it behind. Too many bad messages, I assume."

"You're right." Blue's free hand slipped up to her neck. "I guess I forgot in my concern."

"I know, honey," Hazel offered in a comforting tone. "If you find out anything, even the smallest tidbit, please call." She choked out the last two words.

"I will." Blue squeezed her eyes shut. They flickered open as she said, "Sorry to bother you, Aunt Hazel."

"It's no bother." A sniff carried over the line. "Right now, I feel like you're the only person on my side. You and Buck Adler."

"Buck who?"

"The stranger who bought my property. Yeah, without the money he paid for my house, I'd be stuck here listening to the same old battleaxes spinning lies."

The fact that someone was willing to buy a house in a known flood plain *and* an area where the government would refuse to honor any future flood assistance puzzled her. People bought property because they wanted to live there or they could possibly make a profit from it. Tenny cleared her throat, drawing Blue's attention. Using her index finger, she made a dollar sign in the air.

Understanding her meaning, Blue said, "I hope you got a good price for it."

A weak laugh filled the cab. "*Good* is a relative term. Most people have no use for a two-bedroom cottage with one bathroom. The best I could expect was a little over a hundred thousand if everything worked as it should. Buck offered me a bit more, but the fact he offered anything shocked me. I said yes in a heartbeat."

"*Realtor...*" Tenny whispered the word, not having any hand signals for it. As a reference librarian, she used the web for locating information. The realtor sites served as a wealth of information for how much houses went for in a particular area. Normally, she could pull most information from Zillow, an online realty browsing site, but she doubted even the Zillow people ventured out this far to photograph and list houses. If she had the realtor's name, she could find the price, which might hint at a number of things. Often people from more expensive parts of the country overpaid, expecting similar prices everywhere.

"Did you use a realtor?"

"Lands, no. That would have cost me money. Besides, why should I? We were all expecting to get some money for moving. Buck knocked on my door and asked me if I was interested in selling."

Blue raised her eyebrows. "Weird. Did he say what he wanted the land for?"

"A hunting cabin."

"Weirder still. The area isn't exactly known for hunting."

"That's what I said, but Buck explained once everybody moved out, nature would take over. More trees, plants, deer, and wild turkeys." She clucked her tongue. "I'll miss it. Used to look through the window and see my baby playing outside. She used to be into collecting rocks and crystals. Not so much anymore. She took her various boxes of crystals and returned them to the ground. That's what she called it—basically she threw them into the woods. You think that hunting cabin is legit?"

"Maybe." Tenny voiced her opinion. "All the same, he only owns your house and none of the surrounding land. He couldn't hunt anywhere except around your home."

"That's Tenny," Blue explained into the phone.

"Figured as much. I told him about the same and he explained it wouldn't matter since there would be no one to ask permission from."

"He's right about that," Blue offered.

Tenny ran a hand over her hair and nudged her friend, who said, "Well, I guess we should get going. Got to get home and in a shower

ASAP."

"What did he look like?" Tenny shouted in frustration.

"Young," Hazel answered. "Everyone on the up side of forty resembles a baby. He had a beanie on and glasses. Taller than me, and sounded like a college boy."

"Thanks. Anything else?"

"Can't think of anything."

"Appreciate your trying, Aunt Hazel. Keep in touch and let me know your new address. Good luck!"

"I will. Love you."

"Love you, too."

Blue ended the call and swiveled to face Tenny. "Your opinion?"

"Obviously, the text was sent right before Jess disappeared. As for this Buck stranger, so much is wrong with the hunting cabin scenario." She inserted her fingers into her hair to push her mud-spattered curls off her forehead without luck. "Yuck. I need a shower, like, yesterday."

"Hunting cabin? What's wrong with it? It's odd, I'll admit, considering deer will be wandering through the abandoned Laundromat or Roy's Smokes to Go. It hardly seems fair without decent cover— not very sporting."

"There's that," Tenny replied as she shifted the vehicle into drive and depressed the gas pedal. "Truth is, if the government paid for the land, it belongs to them."

"Hmm…" Blue pressed her lips together, creating the sound of pondering. "If it *is* prone to flooding, what does the government do with it?"

"They could label it a passive nature park or a wildlife sanctuary, which would make hunting an absolute no-no. Sometimes, government land becomes a recreational area for boating, hiking, and camping. Other times, it can be leased out as grazing land. All those scenarios make Buck's plan to have a hunting cabin not workable. Besides, he's paid for land that's already been purchased by the government. I didn't want to say anything about the house, especially if your aunt hasn't received any money and no contract was drawn up. At this point, it could all just be talk. Of course, you do have to wonder why."

"Oh no…" Blue lifted her hands to her face. "Should I call Aunt Hazel and warn her? I certainly don't want her to get in any trouble."

A pothole grabbed Tenny's attention as she carefully maneuvered around it and a frog who hopped in front of the bookmobile. "There sure are a lot of frogs around here."

"People call it a plague of frogs. Rising water makes ponds where there never were any before—prime frog breeding spots, I assume. What should I do about Aunt Hazel?"

"Depends." Tenny scratched her right eyebrow. "There's so much we don't know. Who is Buck Adler? Why does he want Hazel's property? Was any money exchanged or is there only the promise of money? Is your aunt the type to make up stories to justify her sudden exit from town?"

No response from her friend had Tenny glancing from the road to her companion, who sat with a furrowed brow and a grim expression.

"Blue?" Tenny prompted.

An audible exhale served as a reply. "I wish I knew. My mother used to tease Aunt Hazel about some whoppers she told when they were kids. That's been decades ago. Even so, people known for elaborating on fact can still tell the truth and have people not believe them. I just don't want to see my aunt in prison."

"You won't," Tenny promised, unaware if she could keep it from happening.

"Or on the lam," Blue continued. "Constantly changing names and appearance." She paused and pursed her lips. "Aunt Hazel might like that aspect. She always had a flair for the dramatic."

Those who long for excitement often regret it when it arrives in unexpected packaging. "Research saves many from making impetuous decisions."

"Ha!" Blue snorted. "Says the reference librarian. Out here, being able to research anything without adequate Internet service or a library is not a real possibility. If anyone can unravel this predicament, you can. Now, let's go get my bundle of love."

"All righty." Tenny kept her answer to two words while her mind played mental badminton with all her unvoiced thoughts. Why was she supposed to unravel a possible illegal transaction along with finding Jess? Wasn't this trip supposed to be a dry run to see how the bookmobile performed? On that matter, it guzzled gas and was easily stymied by potholes. As for Blue and her troubled relatives, she knew she'd do her best. Hopefully, it would be enough.

Chapter Twelve

THE DARK CLOUDS crowded together like hens in a coop yard fighting over the same bit of corn. Only in their case, Tenny assumed the target must be located on top of the van since no matter how far they drove, the clouds traveled with them, waiting for an opportunity to release their watery bounty.

After her failed attempt to reach her cousin, Blue just stared at the phone in her hand, not speaking. The fact that a twenty-year-old woman left her cell phone when she rushed out canceled any hopes of contacting her. Most people, like her aunt Cinnamon, would mention something about pay phones being everywhere and dropping a dime to make a call. Nowadays, it would take at least two quarters if a person could even *find* a public phone. Then, of course, a person would have to know the number they were trying to call. It was very convenient having the numbers already programmed into their phones. The jagged edges of the scrap paper with a number scribbled across it took shape in her mind.

"Blue," she called softly, waiting until her companion's head jerked before continuing. "I spotted a number in Jess' bedroom. No name or anything on it." She shrugged, wondering why the scrap felt important. "Not sure what it was for. Could be the number of some guy she met?"

A snort greeted the comment. "Come on. How old are you? I don't remember the last time I saw someone physically write down a number." Blue crinkled her nose. "Can you?"

"Put that way, I can't. Someone usually texts you, then you have their number. Often people hand their phones over for it to be put in for them. Still, she left the paper in a visible place for someone to see. Most likely, her mother."

"Maybe..." Blue pursed her lips. "You know, if she darted out, it could be she forgot all about the number."

"Still..." Tenny stalled on the word, trying to decide how to explain a gut feeling just as significant as Jess' not taking anything with her. Good detectives prevailed because they often went with their instincts as opposed to a hard lead. "It can't hurt to give it a try. If it's a friend, maybe they might know where she is."

"Hand it over." Blue put out her hand.

"It's on my phone, which is in the console." Blue flipped up the console lid and rooted through it as Tenny continued, "I didn't feel right taking the number. Just shot a photo of it."

"Good thinking," Blue offered, holding up a pair of scissors and some duct tape along with the phone. "You have a little bit of everything in here."

"Nothing I needed today. Duct tape does come in handy in a number of situations. Uncle Mark used duct tape in both household and automotive repairs. Those particular scissors saved me from squirting catsup all over my car trying to open those fast food packets. Call the number."

"On it." Blue balanced two phones on her lap. "What should I say?"

"She's your cousin. Talk to her like you would normally."

"Um, right," Blue answered while typing the number into her phone.

"Put it on speaker," Tenny instructed. It would be a nice ending to a day to at least find Jess and get her take on the whole situation.

The phone rang three times and then an automated message came on stating the number and asking for a message to be left after the beep. Both women glanced at each other, and Tenny shrugged as a reply.

Blue cleared her throat as the beep sounded. "Hey, this is Blue. Call me. Right away. Bye."

She ended the call. "How was that?"

"Hard to say. It depends on if Jess has memorized your number."

"Oh no!" Blue redialed the number and repeated her message, this time including the number. She sighed and added, "There. I did it."

"Good. All we have to do is wait. Who knows? She might call back and tell us everything has been a huge mistake."

"That would be a relief." Blue sank back into her seat and closed her eyes as Tenny pondered the subject aloud.

"You know that number might not be for Jess' new burner phone. It could be someone else entirely."

"Oh my!" Her hand covered her mouth. "I just left my number."

"It's not a big deal. If it is Jess' number, she'll call you back. If it's a friend of hers, then he or she might ask her to call you."

Blue's hand dropped. "Yeah, not a big deal. Did I even say Jess' name?" She slapped her open hands on her cheeks and exclaimed, "How can anyone know who I'm trying to reach? Maybe I should call again?"

Before Tenny could speak, Blue pushed redial and held up the phone to her ear. "Jess, it's me again. Your cousin, Blue. Call me. Here's my number if you don't have it with you." She rattled off the number. "Please call me right away."

No music and no conversation made the ride to the kennel unusually quiet. Neither woman wanted to miss Blue's phone ring. Never mind that Blue had bumped the volume up to high and vibrate. Doubt about the possibility of missing the vital call crowded the front cab with them as if a third passenger. If intention alone could make the phone ring, it would have burbled miles back. The bright new sign with a smiling dog on it announced the kennel was ahead.

"Thank goodness," Tenny murmured. "I might even be glad to see Sir Moolah."

"Aha!" Blue nudged her friend. "See? He's growing on you."

"Not really. Once he's in the bookmobile, I'll be that much closer to a bath and relaxing with an episode of *Monk*."

"*Monk*? Really? Hasn't that show been off forever? I'd think you'd have seen every episode by now."

"I have. Reruns are on at six p.m. on weeknights. Watching it makes me feel close to Aunt Cinnamon and Uncle Mark. We used to try to solve the crime before Monk did. His superpower was his attention to the smallest thing. Sometimes, a crime could be solved by knowing where a particular flashlight came from. After that, it's *Columbo*. Thank goodness they put in the satellite dish. It gives me something other than the farm report."

The boxy kennel building came into view along with a silver Mercedes parked in the handicapped spot. Blue pointed at the luxury car. "Is that who I think it is?"

How likely would it be for her high school nemesis to show up in another town at a dog kennel when she didn't even own a dog? Not likely at all. She maneuvered the bookmobile past the vehicle, glancing at the license plate and groaning. "Do you think someone else has a vanity plate that reads HOT CHX?"

"It would have to be HOT CHX2 since there can only be one vanity plate of a particular word combination. You stay inside the book-mobile. I'll go get my pup and get the deets on why Rita and possibly her henchwoman, Shadow, are here."

"Not going to argue with you on that point. I only wish I had curtains on the cab like RVs do. That way I could hide behind them." She parked the vehicle facing away from the Mercedes. It was hard to believe one person could intimidate her the way Rita did. As the only child of influential, wealthy parents, Rita exercised her power as a big fish in a small town. Her father had money in various local interests, including owning the building the former Emerson Library rented. What Rita wanted, Rita got, never mind the collateral damage involved.

"Understandable." Blue leaned forward and flicked a bit of mud from Tenny's cheek. "You've looked better. We both know she's after you for having the audacity to date Dallas, her ex. I'll take the flack for you. After all, she's not after my sweetie."

"Thanks, bestie."

"You know, you can move into the back since there are no windows there."

"Yeah." Tenny scoffed. "I'm not afraid of Rita. Not in any mood to see her, but not afraid."

"Whatever," Blue called out and opened the door. "Be back in two shakes of a cow's tail."

Before Tenny could point out it was two shakes of a *lamb's* tail, Blue had closed the door. It didn't matter, since Blue could make any saying bovine-related. That aspect she rather envied in her friend—the ability not to care what others thought.

As far as others' opinions, there was little she could do. People would think what they would, no matter how untrue it might be. Why was her personal gossipmonger and hometown diva here? Didn't she have an insurance company to run? Perhaps she resorted to cold calls now. *Rita work?* Those two words never went together. Sometimes, she played at having a business, but it never lasted long. Anyone who foolishly signed up with her agency would find themselves in a world of hurt if they expected any type of service.

She might as well check for fallen books. After squeezing back into the library area, Tenny sniffed and then grimaced. She cracked the side door open but kept the steps folded up. Some airflow might freshen things a bit. The steps folded down would give the impression that the bookmobile was open for business. Voices drifted in with the breeze. Blue's, she recognized, along with the kennel owner's.

"Ciao!" Rita sang out. Currently, she included foreign words in everyday conversation. Perhaps she thought it gave her international allure.

Leave now, leave now, Tenny mentally chanted.

A spate of barking was followed by a shout. "Moo! No! Come back, Moo! Stop!"

Certain Blue and the dog whisperer could handle it, Tenny

pushed the door wide and stuck her head out. The scruffy pooch chased after Rita, who awkwardly trotted to her car in skyscraper heels. While the sight may have pleased her for a second, she knew it wouldn't end well. Rita reached the sanctuary of her car, slid in, revved the engine, and reversed—making no effort to watch out for Sir Moolah. Blue screamed and Tenny leaped from the bookmobile, forgetting about the stairs, catching one toe on the folded stairs and hitting the pavement hard. Vibrations shot up her hands and arms, even rattling her teeth. She shook her head slowly, trying to orient herself as Rita made a big loop, coming close to Tenny. The power window buzzed down as the car stopped mere feet from her. Rita clicked her tongue. "You constantly amaze me. Just when I think you can't look any worse or be any clumsier, you manage. There's a village somewhere missing its idiot."

Cutting repartee wasn't Tenny's thing. Too bad because she needed something. *Anything.* Sir Moolah trotted over to her and licked her face while Blue yelled at the departing car, "I'm glad my dog didn't bite you. I wouldn't want him to get sick."

Chapter Thirteen

MARVIN TUCKED HIS thumbs underneath the bib of his overalls and angled his head in the direction Rita's car took. The scraggly pines shielded the road, but Tenny would bet even if they hadn't there wouldn't be a glint of silver on the road. She pushed up on the blacktop and untangled her legs from the bookmobile steps as she grumbled, "I imagine she's halfway home by now. Speed limits mean nothing to her." Once Tenny gained her feet, she looked to Blue, who stood cradling her pup in her arms. "Do I sound bitter?"

"Yeah…" Blue grinned, then winked. "I'd say you've earned the right to be a little out of sorts today."

"Just a little?" She brushed her hands together, loosening the pebbles and pine needles embedded in her palms.

"Okay. A *lot*. Do you need any help?" She put out a hand while binding Moolah's squirming body next to her own with the other hand.

"Hold onto that dog! That's how you can help." The last thing she needed was to engage in another chase with the runaway Sir Moolah. Obviously, the dog didn't know when he had it good. Perhaps he might be trying to get back to his original family like so many of the movie dogs. If they ever made a movie about him, they'd have to pick someone with a super annoying voice.

"Got him," Blue assured and wrapped her other arm around the dog in question.

Marvin cleared his throat. "Ah, I hope you won't think less of me as far as dog training goes."

"Oh, no," Tenny started, glancing at the dog and then at Marvin. "What you have here is a *challenge*."

Blue narrowed her eyes and sniffed but didn't dispute the obvious.

"Well," Marvin glanced down at the ground, continuing in a raspy tone, "I promised training, but I hardly had a chance before that woman showed up. Not certain what she wanted. She had me walking all over the place and showing her things. I don't mind doing that if I understand the reason why." He shook his head slowly. "She certainly wasn't here to see me. I might be a decade too old for her. She's more my son's age." He smirked. "My son, Lloyd, isn't hard on the eyes, as the young girls like to say."

"Not sure if they say that anymore," Tenny offered with a slight smile. "Get your point, though."

Marvin grimaced. "I'd warn my son off her—he has enough issues. His bank handled the missing Rivertown funds." He shook his head and cleared his throat. "Anyhow, your friend..."

A groan escaped Tenny at the word *friend* in reference to Rita, but it didn't stop Marvin.

"Ya know, she just wouldn't leave, just kept talking about kennels and doggy daycare. You don't think she's going to start up a competitive kennel nearby?"

Both Tenny and Blue shouted "*No!*" in unison.

"You two got some strong feelings on the matter," Marvin teased. "All the same, I can't figure out what she wanted. I'm just a simple farmer who happens to like dogs."

Talk about a puzzle. Tenny tried to put herself in a Rita mindset. The first thing that occurred to her was the woman came without her sidekick. Who would run her errands and agree with all her statements? That in itself was odd. "Did she try to sell you insurance?"

"Let me see." Marvin pulled off his green John Deere cap and ran his hand over his smooth dome as he pondered the situation. "Can't remember. On the nosy side, even by country standards, she wanted to know how much the Canine Stampede cost to build, which is why I thought she might be planning on building her own."

"Never," Blue declared, rolling her eyes. "Oh, she might talk about it, but I guarantee no one in our town would abuse their animals by taking them there. And if they did, the animals would run away."

"Uh-huh," Marvin agreed, replacing his cap. "I got that feeling myself. All the same, she just stayed, almost as if she were waiting for someone. She looked at her watch several times but stayed. Makes a person wonder."

"I hear you," Tenny replied, while part of her brain turned over what her least favorite person would be doing so far from home. The other part of her brain pointed out her bruised, muddy, and damp state, which made her next decision a no-brainer. "Well, it's time for us to hit the road. Thanks for keeping Moolah for us. We hope to see you again."

"I appreciate it," Blue added. "Next time, we will make sure you get to train him. We can only hope Rita doesn't make a return visit."

Marvin chuckled. "Amen to that."

Blue waved to Marvin and climbed in the passenger side, cradling Moolah while Tenny secured the steps and entry door before scampering into the driver's seat. She gave a playful honk as they drove off. Not even asking for directions, she turned left, listening to the siren song of a hot bath calling her name. When they'd driven for about five minutes, Blue spoke. "Why do you think Rita *was* here?"

"It can't be good." Her lips pulled into a frown as she considered possibilities. "We all know Rita only does things that will benefit her."

"And torment others," Blue remarked.

"That, too." She mulled over the torment part. "Even when she badmouths someone or has her lackey do it, it still benefits her. Like at the café, when Shadow insisted the only reason Dallas would date me was out of pity. In a way, that was supposed to boost Rita's reputation. If Dallas just went out with me because he wanted to, that would make me…"

Blue dramatically gasped and added, "As good as her!" She wiggled her eyebrows. "Actually better, since Dallas made sure to get shed of Rita. It's odd she doesn't run down Dallas' reputation."

"I hadn't thought about that, but you do have a point." A raindrop hit the windshield, followed by several of its relatives. Tenny's heavy sigh filled the cab. "In the summertime, when we need rain, we get nothing. Now that everything has been harvested, it rains non-stop."

"You say that as if you don't actually live here."

"Some things I forgot, like how predatory Rita can be. I worry about Marvin. What could her motives be? Notice she came alone? What do you think of that?"

"No witnesses."

"Murder!" Her foot crushed the brake, bringing the vehicle to a shuddering stop and resulting in a frenzy of canine barking.

"Goodness, Tenny," Blue exclaimed with an amused expression. "You woke up poor Moolah." She fussed over the dog, petting him, and settled him back on her lap before continuing the conversation. "You've been watching too many crime dramas. Rita is very concerned about appearances. As Queen Bee, she knows there are plenty who'd love to see her humiliated. Whatever she was up to, she wanted to keep secret."

That made sense. "You don't think she's planning on opening her own kennel? I lost my library because her father basically closed down our library using his position as president of the chamber commerce just so his daughter could use the space for her insurance agency. She hasn't even been an insurance agent for a month. I have to say it certainly didn't strike me as a career option that suited her personality."

Blue scoffed. "Please. I doubt our hometown diva would have anything to do with animals except for picture opportunities." Sir Moolah curled up on her lap, fell asleep and snored. She brandished an index finger. "I think she was there to meet someone."

"Why do you think that?" Tenny drove on but made a mental note not to slam on the brakes again no matter what the conversation. Tiredness contributed to her impulsive brake slam.

"We went on Marvin's tour. It doesn't take more than fifteen minutes and yet Rita stays. Sounds like she was waiting for someone."

"What about the nosy questions?"

"It's Rita."

"You got that right. She left immediately after we showed up."

"Hmmm," Blue murmured. "I'd pay money to know who she was waiting for."

"Me, too." Tenny sighed. "If only to warn the person."

Chapter Fourteen

WITH THE RAIN ended and the challenging potholes diminished, Tenny relaxed her grip on the steering wheel and half listened to her friend's bookmobile launch plan. A few stray sunbeams had her reaching for her sunglasses. Since the town of Emerson no longer had a library, thanks to Rita's daddy basically evicting the library in favor of his daughter's insurance business, her first soft opening would be her own hometown, Emerson.

The local readers devoured the current library books more than once. Thank goodness she bought more—at least they'd have new reading matter for their perusing pleasure. Even though the thought cheered her, another crowded in right behind, bumping the moment of happiness to the side. Those who'd never supported the library would show up and complain. The bookmobile blocked traffic— what little there was. It's mural of children reading on a sun drenched grassy hill was garish and didn't suit the town color scheme of sun-faded brown. Her back molars snapped together as she pictured a couple of the town's curmudgeons showing up and verbally trashing the idea of a library on wheels. One might insist it wasn't big enough. Rationality never played a part in general grumbling. Before she could ask Blue her opinion, her friend yelled, "Watch out!"

Tenny blinked, not noticing a single vehicle on the road. What was Blue's issue? Then she noticed frogs leaping across the roads. Bullfrogs, medium-size frogs, and even tiny frogs in a ragged procession hopped from one side to the other. Her foot stomped on the brake and books thumped together, a few hitting the floor. The bookmobile shuddered to a stop only a few feet from the frog parade.

Thankful that she'd stopped in time, Tenny's fingers on her free hand slipped up and rubbed her stiff neck while she reassured herself, they were almost home. Never mind it being a lie, but it comforted her. "Where are all the frogs coming from? Did we suddenly merit a plague of frogs?"

"Dunno." Blue tapped her chin and then offered, "Population explosion?" She leaned forward, peering out the windshield. "Look at the one on the end. He's limping." She shot Tenny a look. "The poor dear."

A flustered Tenny felt the need to point out, "I didn't hit him."

"Oh, I know you didn't." Blue grimaced. "He won't survive on his own."

"Circle of life..." Tenny repeated the phrase her uncle Mark often employed to explain animals dying. This came from the same person who brought home a half-starved baby raccoon, which demonstrated he didn't hold to it for everything.

"Here." Blue held out Moolah to Tenny.

She accepted the dog and watched her friend slide out the passenger side. There was no need to ask what her intentions were—Tenny knew. She'd do her best to rescue the compromised frog, and maybe even nurse it back to health. That would mean she'd have two animals in the bookmobile with her preference being none. The frogs bounded away at Blue's exit. A few even went back the way they came, seeking shelter in the underbrush—all except the injured one, freezing in place as if that might save him. It depended on what he needed saving from—fast moving trucks or a wildlife rescuer determined to improve his quality of life.

Blue shed her lightweight jacket and dropped it over the amphibian, scooping him up. What luck it had, if it were bad or good, the next twenty miles would tell. A triumphant Blue entered the truck, beaming with satisfaction. "Caught him!"

"I saw."

As soon as Blue settled into her seat, closed the door, and adjusted her squirming rescued frog bundle, Sir Moolah made an effort to break free. He made no secret of his interest in the newest member of the road trip crew. His dog nails sunk into Tenny's thigh in an attempt to use it as a springboard and launch himself at the frog.

"Ouch!" Tenny tightened her hold on Moolah as her eyes roamed the interior for a frog container. *Nothing.* It must be on her list of things she forgot to bring. She'd pencil *frog container* right under *change of clothes.* "You're going to have to let that frog go."

"He'll die." Blue's voice broke a little, just this side of crying, but trying not to.

Her kind-hearted bestie sometimes took things a trifle too far. Friends and family often bent backward so as not to disappoint the normally bubbly woman. Uncle Mark confessed once that Blue's parents replaced her fish Goldy over a dozen times because they didn't want to break her heart. Now Tenny would have to be the big meanie. She'd tell her it was the frog or the dog and she kinda hoped she'd go for the frog since it was smaller and easier to control.

"It's obvious your frog friend won't survive Sir Moolah. I refuse to drive while wrestling with a dog. It's got to be one or the other." Tenny inhaled and pressed her lips together, trying to look stern—the same expression she used when female students asked her if she knew the address of a certain handsome instructor who had them all aflutter. Never mind that she knew his address, cell phone number, and email address since it was all in the staff registry. Instead, she gave them a simple "No."

"What if I find a container for Fred?" Blue asked with a hopeful expression.

Mercy. She'd already named him. "I looked. There aren't any."

"Let me look. You give up too easily."

Tenny might as well let her discover there was no frog aquarium hidden in the fiction section, and then let her bid Fred a tearful goodbye. "All right. You can look, but at least let me get the bookmobile out of the way."

Once the emergency blinkers were on, Fred and Blue slipped into the back while Tenny held onto a squirming canine. "You know, it's okay to let Fred go. He's a wild creature."

"He's a hurt creature that needs TLC and he'll be as good as new. Then he can go back to being wild."

"He could have gotten hurt..." Tenny stopped before she almost said *being wild*. Griffin would never forgive her if she was the reason behind a frog joining their household.

"Aha!" Blue's voice carried. "Found it."

"Found what?" A sense of resignation settled over her. Their bookmobile clan kept growing.

"A box," Blue declared, squeezing back into the front with the jacket-wrapped frog in one hand and the box in the other. "All I need to do is make some air holes."

A couple of minutes later, Fred relaxed in his new home near Blue's feet. Once the click of the seatbelt sounded, Tenny passed over Sir Moolah, who Blue accepted with open arms and a smile. "How's Momma's other baby?"

Instead of covering Blue with grateful kisses, he lunged for the box, but Blue held him tight. Fred and Moolah wouldn't be featured in online photos with the caption reading *Unusual Friends*. The entire ride back to Emerson, Moolah barked, howled, and tried to get to Fred. A couple of times Tenny's phone burbled. There was no reason to pick it up because she wouldn't be heard over the racket.

No one was happier to see the Emerson town sign announcing *1001 Happy People Live Here!* Talk about a lie. They didn't have a thousand and one people. It would be a stretch to say those they had were happy. Most were content, which worked. "Hey, almost to your truck!" Tenny sang out, realizing she could qualify as happy at the moment.

"None too soon," Blue offered, trying for a smile, which failed. "I think I need to take Marvin up on his offer to train Moo."

"It has merit." Even though a random stranger would probably label Moolah as an ill-behaving dog, Blue wouldn't. Tenny pulled up beside the Holstein-spotted truck, giving her friend enough room to make her transfer. "Door-to-door service," she teased.

"I noticed." She pulled her keys out of her pocket, firmed her grip on Moo, and exited the vehicle. Tenny watched with a sense of relief and anticipation as Blue got in her truck and started it up, knowing a certain bathtub called her name, when she noticed Fred's container on the floor. A *ribbit* confirmed Fred's alive status. "Wait!" she called, but Blue had reversed and headed for home, apparently unaware she'd forgotten her latest project.

Without the dog's constant barking, the lack of noise hung heavy like a wet quilt until her phone rang. It must be Blue, calling to say she was turning around.

"Hello? Coming back for your frog?"

"Frog?" Dallas' voice filled her ear. He gave a slight chuckle and added, "I never had a frog. Is this code?"

"No." She blew out a long breath. "Blue had to rescue this lame frog and now she left him with me."

"That's bad."

"I thought so, too."

"Raccoons eat frogs. You should know that, Miss Reference Librarian."

Tenny closed her eyes, wondering if she had made the mistake of thinking *what else could happen*? She knew better than to tempt fate. "Of course, I do. I just didn't think I would be frog-sitting. All the more reason Blue needs to get her frog. For now, I'll keep Precious and Fred apart."

"Fred?" Dallas repeated the name.

"The frog."

"Blue named him."

"Yep."

"That doesn't bode well."

"Tell me about it. Right now, I need to get into the house and scrape the first layer of mud off me."

"Should I ask?"

"Don't." Tenny shook her head as if Dallas could see. "Maybe I could call you back later?"

"I'd like that."

She bid him goodbye while wondering how to bring up the topic of his toxic ex, Rita. Most people don't want to talk about their exes and their activities, suspicious or otherwise. "C'mon, you know you'd love for Rita to be guilty of some skullduggery." Well aware some people considered talking to themselves one of the first signs of losing it, she added, "Isn't that right, Fred?"

The frog stayed silent regarding his opinion.

Chapter Fifteen

THE WATER SLOWLY gurgled into the tub as Tenny rushed around gathering clean clothes and towels. Shampooing her hair would be a must, along with cutting her nails. Mud had seeped in everywhere when she acted as a lever for the bookmobile. She'd probably inhaled a fair amount, too. She would treat that by drinking copious amounts of water. Just to be safe, she shook some cereal into a pie pan and put it outside for Precious' dinner. If she was eating cereal, Precious could, too.

All the same, she refused to discount the raccoon's ability to get into places where he should not and brought Fred's box into the bathroom. Once free of mud, she'd head down to the hardware store that sold bait and buy some earthworms for Fred's dinner. Even if she didn't make it before five, the current owner of the store lived next door and would open up for a sale. Her lips pursed as she considered the possibility of Blue's returning for her forgotten amphibian. "Nah. I'd better spring for the earthworms. Otherwise, Fred might die from hunger."

He *could* die from a number of things, but Blue would insist it was hunger, which would mean Tenny bore the blame for not providing an appropriate diet. She carried in the portable radio along with her cell phone, hoping to get in some multi-tasking while trying to separate herself from the residue of an awful day.

She tested the water with her hand and added a little more cold. Curious about Fred, she lifted one panel and peeked into the cardboard box. The frog huddled in a corner, his sides moving with his breathing, looking dehydrated to her untrained eyes. Perhaps water would revive him. Not certain how a frog would react to the well water, Tenny put a shallow cool two inches of water into the stoppered sink and scooped up Fred and placed him gently into the water. She'd swear the frog sighed as it entered the water.

Maybe it didn't sigh, but she did as she eased her aching body into the warm water. Tomorrow, muscles she never used would scream about abuse. The bottle of bath gel emitted sucky noises as she squeezed it, indicating its almost empty state. Not willing to exit her comfortable bath and search for more bath gel, which she probably wouldn't find, she pushed the bottle under water and squeezed again, then released, allowing it to suck up water and create a greatly reduced soapy solution, but a solution all the same.

She closed her eyes, luxuriating in doing nothing for a few seconds—simple inhaling and exhaling, focusing on her breathing the way meditation videos urged you to do. Think of thoughts as balloons and let them drift away. Only, her thought balloons huddled together and burst, ruining her moment of peace.

After scrubbing her skin pink, she reached for her cell phone and pressed a key for her voice mail. A robotic female voice let her know she had eight messages. After placing it on speaker, she held it with her hand outside the tub. She rested her head on the rim of the slipper tub, trying to reclaim her ease.

The first message was from a collection agency, trying to reach a Melissa. Tenny blew out a breath. "Not them again." When she received her cell phone number, she also inherited a number of debt collectors with the number. She deleted the call.

The next call began with silence, then a throat clearing, then a male voice. "Hey, Tenny! Long time no see."

The voice sounded familiar, but it had been a few months. "Andrew." She murmured the name of her former on-and-off boyfriend. Odd he chose to call. Maybe he called as a condolence once he heard her aunt died.

"It's Andrew." He gave a weak laugh. "In case you don't remember. We should get together. Call me." Another delete.

Weird. His voice brought with it the reminders of her old life, working at the university library, living alone in her studio apartment, and getting together with her librarian friends for trivia night at a local bar and grill. Librarians ruled when it came to trivia. Usually, a pang occurred whenever she considered her former life, but not today. Strange, considering her day's activities.

The phone clicked, signaling another message, a hesitation, and then a woman's low, whispery voice. "You need to move the bookmobile. You're not licensed for a business." Then silence. Yep, a definite delete. Who could be so hateful to rag on the bookmobile? An image of her nemesis came to mind. It could be her or someone she coerced into doing her bidding. Her fingers hovered over the keyboard as she considered deleting, but didn't. The phone dropped to the fluffy blue rug only a few inches away as she loosened her grip on it.

Enough crime dramas demonstrated how deleted messages could have proven harassment or even motivation for murder. She hoped the second one wouldn't be an issue. She grabbed the shampoo bottle, dunked her hair into the water, and vigorously lathered before dunking again.

Rinsed and free of mud, she realized she hadn't played all her messages, too concerned about little Miss Hateful/Shadow trying to disguise her voice. As for businesses that ran out of homes, she could name a half dozen on her road alone. Counting off on her fingers, she listed aloud, "There's Bettina's Curl and Nails, Lorinda's Playhouse Day Care, Tammy Lee charges people ten dollars a visit to use her tanning bed, and Grandma Esther made fruitcakes in the winter, noodles in the fall, and pickles in the summer for sale. Then there's all the direct sales parties for sportswear, candles, storage wear, and kids' toys. So, are those people guilty of running a business in a place not zoned for businesses? That's why people move to the country to get away from all those regulations."

Tenny retrieved her phone to finish listening to her messages.

"Ribbit," Fred added, placing his webbed hands on the edge of the sink and peering over.

Tenny glanced up from her phone just in time to see her amphibian visitor push off into a downward leap. "Oh no!"

She dropped her phone with a watery plop and surged forward with both hands to catch a slippery Fred. Half in and half out of the tub, she cradled the frog in her hands. "Well, it's easy to see why you got hurt in the first place. You don't make good decisions. You need to think things through."

He croaked again either in agreement or complaint.

"Yeah, I know." She placed the frog carefully down on the floor and pushed up to exit the bathtub properly. The colorful rectangle floating in the tub at first confused her, but then she recognized it. "My phone!"

A quick scoop netted her phone, which she wrapped in a towel.

Then she wrapped herself as she stepped out of the tub. "Rice. That's what I need." She swung the bathroom door in search of the staple that had rescued many cell phones over the years. The only problem was she'd be without cell service for at least twenty-four hours. Considering her most recent calls, it wouldn't be much of a loss.

As she rooted through the cupboard, she heard the sound of a wet *plop*. Her lips pursed as she considered the sound. "Fred!"

Her froggy visitor was on the loose due to her forgetting to close the bathroom door. "First things first." She shivered a little as she ripped open the bag of rice, poured it into a bowl, then disassembled her phone, pushing it deeply into the rice.

An audible exhale escaped as she considered her next urgent task. Find Fred.

Before she could, a knock sounded on her front door. Who could that be? Tenny hot-footed to the bathroom, struggled to pull Uncle Mark's robe onto her damp body, sashed it, finger-combed her hair, and hoped only Blue waited at the front entrance. A peek out the front window revealed no one.

It could be they stomped off because she took so long to answer. She hesitated, her hand on the door. What if UPS delivered the books she ordered? Talk about a ray of sunshine. She swung open the door smiling, and in an effort to locate the box, pushed open the screen door—which unfortunately was wide enough for Precious, who dashed inside. "Precious!" She mumbled his name in disgust, realizing she'd again been played by a raccoon. Galloping behind that emotion rushed another one as she yelled "Fred! Hide!"

Chapter Sixteen

TENNY HELD HER breath as Precious lowered his head and sniffed a bug-eyed Fred, who stared at the predator unblinking. *Remember, raccoons are omnivores who happen to eat frogs. After all, my original plan involved his returning to the wild to hunt his own food.* Technically, she couldn't be too mad about his doing what raccoons do. All the same, she debated about rushing him, but with her luck, she'd end up stepping on Fred.

For one second, then two, the animals regarded each other with fixed gazes. Precious then sauntered over to Tenny, tugged on her robe hem, and chattered away. Normally, she'd call it indecipherable, but today not so much.

"Okay," Tenny answered. "I will make you scrambled eggs. Gladly. As long as you recognize that Fred isn't dessert." Not willing to test Precious, she waited until he moved away, scooped up Fred, and put him back into the box, which she carried with her. No box, closed or otherwise, deterred a determined raccoon.

As she whipped up the egg froth, she considered how her aunt's spoiling Precious certainly worked in Fred's favor. No way would this raccoon go for raw food when he could have it cooked to order. Fred's box sat on the counter arm's length from the stove. The heated iron skillet gave off a sizzle as the eggs touched the surface.

Using a wooden spoon, Tenny chased the bubbling mixture around, turning it to prevent burning. When finished, she scraped it into Precious' bowl resting on the counter and added two ice cubes for cooling purposes.

Excited about the possibility of cooked food, Precious rocked back on his hind quarters and held out his front hands as if beseeching Tenny. She could almost hear his little animal voice with a proper British accent saying, "Please, may I have some more?" while holding up an empty bowl.

"Let it cool. Don't want to burn your dainty mouth." She stopped halfway in the process of filling up his water dish. Did she just call Precious' mouth dainty? Most people referred to raccoons as trash pandas for their habit of dining on garbage. The water dish sloshed a little as she placed it on the floor. Precious ambled over to it, cocking his head and giving Tenny a meaningful stare.

"Demanding," she declared and put down the food dish. "Hurry up and eat. I have to get dressed and mosey down to the hardware store."

She did just that as Precious relished his meal. Not trusting the masked bandit, she carried Fred's box with her. Suitably attired in jeans, a long-sleeved T-shirt that announced *Book Boyfriends Are the Best*, and a worn pair of Ked tennis shoes, she bunched her curls into a sloppy bun and pushed on her glasses. Knowing she'd see some town folks, she smoothed tinted lip balm over her lips—a hundred percent better than how she looked an hour ago and ready to meet the world.

"Precious, I'll need you to please go outside since I'm heading out." She scooped up Fred's box and glanced over at the raccoon, not expecting much. His tiny hand popped the last egg morsel into his mouth as he turned and wandered up to her and sat. A casual observer might think he responded to her command. Her nose crinkled. Not hardly. The creature always acted as if he were participating in a game of opposites. If she said stay, he left. If she told him to leave, he settled in. To test her theory, she shouldered her purse, picked up Fred's box, and headed toward the front door. "We're leaving. Heading down to the hardware store. Let's go."

Her rubber-soled shoes slapped the floor, but there were no other sounds. On the whole, people didn't hear raccoons until they knocked over a trash can or a flower pot. A backward glance demonstrated that Precious shadowed her steps. She pulled the front door wide, opened the screen door, and waited for Precious to waddle through before closing both doors. She considered locking it, but decided against it. She wouldn't be gone that long and the house was visible from the hardware store. When you got right down to it, the only critter she wanted to keep out of her home kept pace with her.

The three of them made their way down the street attracting waves, which she returned with a grin. A gap-toothed, chubby preschool-age girl begged, "Can I pet your raccoon?"

"Oh, he's not a pet," she assured with a nod. Using her best reference librarian tone, she added, "Precious is a wild creature."

"Oh." The girl glanced at Precious, then back to Tenny. She put one balled fist on her hip, possibly imitating her mother or another adult she'd seen do likewise. "He's got a *name*."

"Yes, he does."

She sucked in her lips and regarded Tenny with a solemn stare. "Grandpa Yoder has goats. Lots of them."

"That's nice for Grandpa Yoder." Growing up as an only child,

Tenny never had much interaction with very young children. From her short time working in the town's library, she discovered the very young often told jokes with missing punch lines and engaged in conversations with no clear endings.

"He didn't give them names."

"Not unusual with livestock."

In the distance, she could see an older woman working her way across the yard. Tenny recognized her as one of Cinnamon's friends—although, that label could apply to most people in town. As Tenny tried to extract the name from her unreliable memory, she glanced at her watch.

Her young questioner failed to notice the watch glance or understand the subtle nuance. Instead, she popped the other hand up on her hip and said with great emphasis, "Grandpa Yoder didn't name the goats because they're not pets."

"He's right," she added, well aware that Blue named every single cow they had and they weren't pets either.

"You named your raccoon. He *must* be a pet."

The dreaded circular reasoning so popular with children and a handful of adults. By this time, the older woman had reached them and heard the last sentence. "She has you there."

The name *Eula* formed on Tenny's lips—not because of great memory, but because she still had her Dollar General nametag pinned to her shirt. "Eula, you know Cinnamon named him. He's not my pet."

"Keep telling yourself that." She grinned so wide her smile lines and crow's feet almost met. "Where you headed?"

"Hardware store."

"Amos's probably still open. You might want to get some of

those flea pills you feed to dogs, too."

"I don't have a..." she started, and then noticed Eula staring at Precious. "I might consider it," she said, amending her statement.

"Glad to hear it. As pet owners, we have to take care of our four-legged friends. Getting Precious a rabies and distemper shot would not only help him but also anyone he might encounter." She placed a hand affectionately on the inquisitive girl's head. "I would hate for my Amanda Sue to be bitten."

"Oh, Precious would never do that." Her attempt at reassurance failed since Eula raised one eyebrow. "All dogs have the potential to bite, just like all cats could scratch you. Raccoons probably have it in their bloodline even more."

Another problem that needed to be dealt with before it blew up into something big. One of the prelaw students who frequented the library informed her that people slapped *Beware of Dog* signs on their fences, thinking it would protect them against any lawsuits. It did just the opposite since it acknowledged they knew their dog was dangerous.

"I will definitely check into shots. Thanks for the advice."

"No problem. I've said the same to Cinnamon. You might check with the local vet and find out if Precious has already had his vaccinations." She chuckled, dropped her hand from Amanda's head, and sighed. "I didn't come over here to lecture you about Precious. I actually wanted to thank you for your perseverance. First, starting our little library, then moving on to the bookmobile. Cinnamon would be so proud. Personally, I approve, too. Heard the more you read to a child, the better they do. I want that for my Amanda Sue. It sure helps to have books I can check out."

"Oh, thank you!" Tenny sputtered the words, overwhelmed with gratitude. "With the day I've had, this means the world to me."

"Glad to help." Eula angled her head in the direction of the box. "May I ask?"

"Hurt frog, but not a pet."

"Yet…" Eula added, chuckling as she guided her granddaughter back to her house.

"Not a pet," Tenny murmured, affirming her intent, hoping to still her own doubts.

Chapter Seventeen

OUTSIDE, FULL NIGHT darkened the horizon, resulting in the whip-poor-wills starting their evening serenade. Even a robin broke into a full-throated song. The falling temperatures sent those used to the hotter summer temps inside. The flickering light of televisions flashed through parted curtains.

A crime drama droned in the background as the police detective in a rumpled raincoat said, "Just one more thing." Tenny snapped out of her half-drowsing state and struggled into a seated position. No way would she miss out on how the clever man solved the crime by observing everyone's footwear. If only it were that easy.

The detective explained in detail what could have happened. He tapped a finger on his temple and added something about his wife telling him to follow the money. Good advice. That's what she and Blue were trying to do, but first, they had to find the money. If they couldn't find the actual money, perhaps they could find a sudden lavish display of spending.

She pulled Fred's box closer and examined the drowsing frog cuddled up on a damp washcloth. With his legs tucked under and his head on the blue cloth, he made a cute picture. Only, Clyde down at the hardware sure didn't think so. Even though the man sold her Fred's dinner and breakfast, he called rehabbing a frog a fool's plan.

Maybe it was. How quickly she'd forgotten how people in small towns shared their opinions whether you asked for them or not.

She rubbed her hands together, trying to dispel the needle-prickling sensation from sleeping on them and contemplated whether she should give Fred another sink treatment. Only this time, she'd be on guard for any escape attempts. The credits rolled across the screen, catching her attention. The clearly guilty construction boss ended up cuffed and riding in the back of a squad car. Television often portrayed the guilty party with a heavy hand—that way no one minded seeing them arrested, but what if the culprit wasn't some embezzler robbing widows and children while living a billionaire lifestyle? What if it were just an ordinary person who made a bad choice?

So far, Jess remained a real possibility. Occam's Razor, a philosophical tool, eliminated convoluted theories by picking the simplest. Most people intent on robbery don't concoct an elaborate scheme—although to them it might appear elaborate. Most were impulsive snatch-and-run types. It also served as the reason they were caught, too.

If she were following the money, like they do on her crime shows, the person with items out of their price range would merit a second look. This would require the names of the council members along with local gossip. Due to the lack of things to do in a small town, the antics of the residents provided limited entertainment. Sure, the big spenders may have qualified for a new credit card or even received an inheritance—that's where gossip helped. Blue's aunt Hazel might not be in the inner circle if she happened to be the target of gossip.

She blew out a breath as she analyzed her next step. The council member's names should be in the local newspaper coverage or online. Somehow, she'd have to meet each person and take their measure and notice any diamond-studded watches on their wrists or expensive sports cars in their driveways. What excuse could she use once she located them?

The landline rang once, then a second time, and finally, a third before Tenny pushed off the couch, carrying Fred's box with her in her phone search. A teetering pile of junk mail almost hid the rotary phone. When she finally found it, it stopped ringing. *Figures.*

The acrid smell of burnt popcorn lingered, causing her to crinkle her nose. Popcorn for dinner turned out to be a bad decision. Aunt Cinnamon's microwave had served her well over the years, but most of the numbers on the cook pad had worn off, which made using it a bit of a guessing game. Before she went to bed, she'd put a bowl of vinegar inside.

"Probably Blue calling me to tell me she forgot Fred. As if I wouldn't have noticed by this time." She addressed the box. "Good news! A more competent pet care specialist will be here soon." Her neck, stiff from her impromptu nap on the couch, resulted in her rolling it around, causing it to snap, pop, and crackle, rather like the cereal.

The phone rang again. Tenny surveyed the kitchen. There was no sign of Precious, which could mean just about anything. Had she let him back in after the hardware trip? After all, she did have Fred beside her on the couch. That could be because she was lonely, too. Certain no Precious waited nearby, she put Fred's box on the dining room table and answered the phone.

"Hello?"

"What took you so long?" A brusque voice inquired.

Tenny pulled the phone from her ear and regarded it the way most people might if the device had transformed into a snake. Blue never yelled or grumbled, and as far as insults went, the best she ever did was so roundabout most people missed it. She called a poorly executed fish fry at the local church cooking oil that could have been put to better use. Anyone else would have called it terrible. "Excuse me?"

"Don't get your hackles up. I heard from Jess or her abductors."

Not sure if she was fully awake, Tenny grabbed a bit of tender skin near her wrist and twisted. "Ouch!"

"What are you doing?"

"Testing a theory. You heard from Jess?"

"Maybe."

"It's either you did or didn't. Which one?"

A long pause ensued and Blue hemmed a little. "I got a text from that number you found."

"So, you *did* hear from her."

Doubt colored Blue's words. "I heard from someone."

"Read me the message." She shot her free hand through her hair, getting it caught in the hair tie that held a few tendrils together.

Blue cleared her throat and read. "I'm fine. Safe. Tell me what everyone is saying. Who do they think took the money?" She paused and then added, "That's it."

"Sounds like Jess?"

"Not to me." She sniffed. "I'm worried."

"You would be." Her lips pursed as she considered the brief message. *Fine* was an odd expression to use if you were in hiding. If she were hiding, would she want to know about people thinking she took the money? *Wait.* Hazel had mentioned something. "Didn't

Hazel say people were sending her nasty texts about stealing the money?"

"She did."

"So, it should be a no-brainer as far as what people are saying. I can see why you think it isn't your cousin."

"Yeah, but that's not it." A long exhale sounded. "About ten years ago, I took Jess to the movies. It was a big deal because she wanted to see this cartoon with this big, bald-headed guy who was supposed to be a supervillain and he ends up adopting these three little girls."

"Doesn't sound very villainy."

"He wasn't—too much. Anyhow, with the girls, I told her she was more like Edith. She used to call me Margo. She'd never start a text without some sort of greeting along those lines. Such as, Hey Margo, it's me, Edith. It was our inside joke."

"Overly stressed people might forget."

"Habit. After so many years, it became a habit. Polite people trying to escape a fire in a public building have said excuse me as they pushed their way out."

Her nose crinkled at her friend's rationale. "She might leave off a greeting if she were texting in a hurry. Asking what people are saying sounds like a fishing expedition, considering she knew what they're saying."

"Good point." Blue's voice almost resumed its normal tone until her next inquiry. "What if her abductor is making her say this?"

Normally, people were kidnapped for ransom or to force someone into a certain action. Occasionally, a stalker could nab the target of his or her obsession. "No request for a ransom or any type of action. We can probably assume it's a number for someone other than Jess. The question is who? Did you text back?"

"Not yet. That's why I called you. What should I say?"

"Ask to meet. That would be the quickest way to determine if it *is* Jess. Ask something only she would know. Use your code words and see if you get the right response. If nothing else, we'll figure out if you're texting a random guy."

"Good advice."

"What about Fred?" Tenny questioned the phone without any response. Blue had already hung up without even saying goodbye, which just went to show people did forget social niceties when stressed.

Chapter Eighteen

CALLS OF *"Go right. No, not that way. The other way. The llama is getting away!"* jostled Tenny awake. Her eyelids slowly opened in the early morning light, and then she closed them. Did she really want to know what was going on? The last few moments luxuriating in bed before getting up served as the most cherished because they were so fleeting. A nearby ribbit reminded her of Fred. She might as well get going. Maybe she could get Fred in to the vet before she fumigated the bookmobile for its hometown debut.

Her eyes open, her vision a little blurry without her glasses, she still made out the shaggy head and long neck of llamas through her slightly parted bedroom curtains. "City people imagine the country as a bucolic paradise," she grumbled as she carried Fred into the kitchen.

She switched out his dry washcloth for a new one, making sure to dribble some water on him in the process. "Most say they want to move to the country for peace and quiet."

A father and daughter team raced by the kitchen window, waving their arms and shouting suggestions about how to round up the footloose and fancy-free mammals, which were possibly a 4-H project. A peek out the front window allowed her to see the llamas had taken to the street, which was good. Neighbors would step out on their stoops and give their opinion on animal wrangling and possibly lend a hand. Good. Otherwise, she'd feel guilty for not helping—not that she knew much about llamas. A dog might join the chase possibly, calling on some long-forgotten herding ancestry.

After filling up the coffee pot, she returned to her original subject as if Fred cared. "Peace and quiet, they say. No traffic. Never mind the escaping animals and the owners hot on their trail. Not an everyday occurrence, but more often than one might expect. Then there's the strawberry cannons and the tractors that start before daylight."

"Ribbit!"

"Yeah, I know, buddy. You want breakfast. Coming up." She swung open the fridge door and located the Styrofoam worm container. No sooner had she fed him his chilled worms, which were a little less wiggly than the previous day, a *rattling* sounded at her back door. Precious.

She scooped up the box before letting the raccoon inside. Part of her voted for cereal for her masked visitor, but another part realized he needed something as appetizing or more so than a living, close-by frog. The heady scent of coffee perfumed the air. Tenny inhaled the aroma. It was not quite the same as drinking it, but it perked her up a little.

Cradling the box against one hip, she awkwardly withdrew the carton of eggs, milk, and butter from the fridge. Stepping around Precious, who stood in the middle of the floor fussing, she managed to retrieve a skillet and a mixing bowl. A few minutes later Precious savored his meal while Tenny sipped her coffee, coming fully awake. She needed to confirm what time the IGA grocery would let her park and open her bookmobile for business. Trulan, the assistant manager, told her one to four would be fine. That way, children could visit after school.

It would have been easier if she'd just parked it at the school. She scoffed at the possibility of easy and slurped her coffee. Why did what she originally thought would be a simple idea take ten separate steps and require a committee to vote on it? At least with the IGA, she had walked in to get bread and ended up asking Trulan for a time she could monopolize a corner of the parking lot. Weekdays worked better than weekends when many did their shopping. Blue promised her supportive presence at the event. Better text and remind her. Where was her phone anyhow?

Done with his food, Precious scampered onto the Formica counter and sauntered toward the bowl of rice with sections of Tenny's cell phone sticking out. "Oh no you don't!"

The sudden image of her phone's descent into the tub and her actions to reclaim it came rushing back. Tenny knocked her chair back and lunged for the bowl before Precious reached it. She'd barely grabbed the bowl in time, sloshing rice onto the floor in the process. "I think it's time for you to appreciate the great outdoors." She herded her hair-covered sibling toward the back door, listening to his objections but not caving to any of them. When she swung the door open, a llama shot into her back yard, startling Precious, who headed deeper into the house. Following close behind the llama was the daughter and a good half-dozen people and a baying beagle.

Ah yes, the silence of a country morning. Too bad she couldn't appreciate it due to all the commotion. Accepting she'd have to locate Precious before she left, she picked up Fred and the box before heading to the bedroom to dress.

By ten that morning, the llamas were caught after trampling more than a few flower gardens, upsetting chickens, and tearing down a couple of clotheslines in the process. Tenny inspected her own yard and picked up the pieces of a broken terra-cotta pot. She held up the jagged pieces. Llama? She shook her head. For the most part, llamas were pretty sure-footed and would have avoided stepping on the pot. More likely it was the horde chasing them that did the damage. Using her shoe, she pushed most of the dirt off the sidewalk. There was no time to sweep since she had snagged a vet appointment due to a cancellation.

Using the landline, she imagined herself back in 2000. Even though many teens possessed bulky cell phones that resembled walkie-talkies and the cutting-edge flip phone, Aunt Cinnamon and Uncle Mark held off buying her a cell phone, stating there was no real reason to have one with the non-existent coverage in Emerson. Those who rushed out to be part of the horde often ended up standing outside on picnic tables or even garage roofs for a good connection. Not exactly the cool image they wanted. Thank goodness she hadn't disconnected the landline. It allowed her to confirm her IGA bookmobile appearance, get an appointment for Fred, and find out more about Precious' vaccinations. She wasn't even going to try to wrestle the raccoon into a carrier only to find out he was current on his shots.

The windows were open on the bookmobile, airing it out after Tenny used a deodorizer on the carpet meant for pet accidents. Why did solutions like that have to smell so bad on their own? Or, it could have been the combination.

A black and white spotted truck approached with Blue half hanging out of the driver's window. "Hey! Hey!"

Tenny waved, forgetting she had a handful of pottery shards. A fine spray of dirt landed on her shirt and glasses. She forcibly exhaled, trying to dislodge it. Not working, she tossed the shards away to find out what had Blue out and about. The pieces rattled as they hit a metal container, but failed to mute Blue's truck door slam. "What in the world are you doing? Giving me heart palpitations."

"You're too young for that."

"I called your cell. Last night. This morning." She pointed at Tenny. "You didn't answer."

"I couldn't. Besides, we talked on the landline. You knew I was okay." She attempted to explain, but her friend continued. Color climbed into her pale cheeks as she crossed her arms. "You were ignoring me because I forgot Fred."

"Forgot?" Tenny echoed the word, making it into a question.

"Yes, I forgot." She pushed a chunk of hair behind her ear. "So much going on with Moolah being his usual escape artist self, and then trying to remember Aunt Hazel's tell because I'm pretty sure she was lying to us. Why didn't you answer?"

"I dropped the phone in the tub." Tenny tried not to smirk as the angry flush left Blue's face, and the good mad she'd built up drained away, leaving her momentarily speechless and pale. Gaining her breath, she said, "Ah! That makes sense."

"You could have called the landline again."

Blue opened her mouth, shut it, and then slapped her thigh. "Should have. Moolah got in the field and started barking at the Holsteins. I had to get out there before one of them kicked him.

Even the best tempered bovines do have a breaking point."

Anyone else might say something about Moolah. Tenny suppressed her initial sympathy for the cow. "Your aunt has a tell?"

"Oh yeah, she does." Blue nodded. "Had to call my mother because I couldn't remember. Apparently, when the two would play cards, if Aunt Hazel had a good hand or maybe she wanted the card on the discard pile and didn't want my mother to take it, she'd pull on her ear."

As tells go that would have been a bit too visible for an observant sibling—but only if a person were looking for it. What about tugging on a too-tight earring, or even scratching your ear, which could be misinterpreted? Tenny considered the possibility. "I don't think I saw her pull her ear."

"Not surprising." Blue jingled her keys as she arched an eyebrow. "You'd have had to have been in the kitchen to notice. You fussed with your books and then, when you did come in, you hightailed it to the…" She stopped and made air quotes with her fingers. "…bathroom."

"Don't forget the beanie wienies lunch. I was there for that. What about you?"

Blue tucked her keys into her jeans pocket and shrugged. "It's hard to tell. Most of the time she had her head in either the freezer or the cabinet. When she was at the stove talking to me, she had her back to me." Her brow furrowed as a grunt escaped her. "I think she did that deliberately. She probably suspected that my mother told me about her tell—since my mother isn't known for keeping things to herself. No wonder she kept turning away from me. Normally, Aunt Hazel is known as a close talker. You know, one of those folks who get so close you have to back up?"

A professor at the university reigned as a close talker. At first, Tenny thought the elderly department head might harbor an affection for her until she heard other staffers complain about his closeness and how you could smell his breath, which usually betrayed his fondness for Italian food. "I know one. So, you think your aunt lied to you?"

"Lie is such an ugly word." Her lips lifted in a lopsided smile. "Normally, she'd be bubbling over with questions and staring you straight in the eyes. She went to one of those inspirational sales conferences where the speaker emphasized the importance of holding eye contact." A small sigh sounded. "After that conference, besides being a close talker, she started keeping constant eye contact. It made me feel like I was being grilled by the FBI at times."

"She certainly didn't act that way when we visited."

"Yeah." Blue placed one hand on her hip. "That's what got me thinking about ear pulling. Did I see any? I can't remember. What I did notice was the lack of eye contact. Feels like she's keeping something from me." Her smile dropped.

"What?"

"Don't have a clue."

"It could be almost anything," Tenny agreed. "Unusual behavior." Maybe that applied to the lunch selection, too. "I did notice one thing."

Blue's hand slipped back to rub her neck. "Go on."

"Well," Tenny started, and then stopped, trying not to think about her own relationship with her mother. Most people considered Cinnamon her mother, but she never asked her to call her Mom—possibly because she knew her sister could turn up at any time. Although Cinnamon and Mark did legally adopt her, that in itself made her wonder. Did they get in contact with her mother to sign the paperwork? There were also all the unopened letters and cards from her mother to her that she'd found in the fire-safe box. Even though her plan was to open them, she hadn't yet. A thickness in her throat resulted in her coughing. "Ah, I was going to say, a mother who's close to her daughter, which I assume Jess and Hazel are…"

"They are," Blue acknowledged.

"Then," Tenny picked up where she left off, "the mother doesn't just move when her daughter is missing. When we were at the house, she acted as if Jess would come home when she was ready. That she wasn't in any jeopardy. She'd acted more upset about people badmouthing Jess than her daughter's actually being gone. Why isn't she contacting the police? Putting flyers up? Driving to all the places Jess might have gone?"

Blue rested one finger against her lips, and then dropped it as she replied with a thoughtful mien. "Griffin asked me if we decided to go to Rivertown on our own, or did Aunt Hazel ask for help."

"It was your idea."

"I know." She slowly surveyed the area before adding, "I may have let Griffin assume we went at the request of Aunt Hazel. Come to think of it, if your child was missing, wouldn't you contact everyone you know, if only to check if they had heard from them?"

"Something feels off. If we could figure it out, we might be closer. You can call your aunt. Fred has a vet appointment, which should be *your* department. All the same, I'm taking him along to find out more about Precious' rabies vaccination. Remember, the bookmobile's soft opening is at the IGA parking lot at one p.m. today. Be there."

Chapter Nineteen

THE MULTICOLORED FLAGS tied across the IGA grocery store flapped in the breeze as the radiant afternoon sun beamed down on the unfolding scene. Trucks flew down the main drag, well aware it was patrolled only on very rare occasions, creating a *swoosh* sound background. An occasional horn protested those who had the nerve to turn into the grocery before swerving around them.

The bookmobile sat at an angle in the lot corner with its entry door propped open and its steps down. Tenny grunted while wrestling a rectangular table through a narrow doorway meant for people and not moving furniture. A metallic clang announced her unsuccessful struggle, with the win going to the table or possibly the door. She glared at both as her lips twisted in disgust. "All I want to do is get the table set up. This is supposed to be easy."

How many times had those same words exited her mouth when faced with yet another obstacle in her path to becoming the roving purveyor of the printed word plus a few digital books? Balancing on the steps, she lowered the table against the lip of the door, which should give her a moment. With any luck, the fairy godmother of good causes would arrive, wave her wand, and all would be well.

"Hey, wait! Let me help," a familiar masculine voice called out.

Dallas, attired in worn jeans, work boots, a straw cowboy hat, and a plaid shirt, exited his pickup. He waved and then dashed her way. Not quite her fairy godmother, but he'd do. Before Tenny could say hello, he grabbed the end of the table that stymied her. With a twist and a pull, it slipped out of the bookmobile like butter.

"Whoa!" She whistled. "Look at you. Experience with bookmobiles?"

"Nope." He flipped the table over, pulled out the legs, and locked them in place before standing it upright with ease. "Camping. My family visited all the national parks reachable by driving. My mother had the campsite set up in ten minutes flat, but it required all of us doing our part."

"Your mother's amazing."

"That's not what I said at the time." He chuckled and ran a hand over his face. "Those were the days. It's funny. When they were happening, I didn't appreciate them. Felt sorry for myself because we weren't going to Disney World or Universal theme park. Need help with anything else?"

"Not really. You've already done all the heavy lifting. I'll arrange the table and wait for people to show up." She stuck out her tongue and added, "I guess I should say *if* people show up."

"Did you advertise?" He made eye contact and cocked his head the tiniest bit, which might not indicate much with anyone else, but with Dallas, it meant he suspected the answer. If the man ever had kids, he'd probably use the same exact gesture when quizzing his teens about what time they came home last night.

"Ah, yeah, I knew I was forgetting something. I put a flyer on the IGA bulletin board. It all happened so fast." She shrugged, well aware she'd done a poor job of planning her first bookmobile stop. "With trying to chase down the culprit who made off with Rivertown's missing money, plus yesterday's dry run in the torrential rain…" Her eyes rolled upward at the memory. "You were right. The wiper blades were dry-rotted."

A huff of agreement came with the mention of the wipers, but Tenny continued, "Anyhow, I may have forgotten." She winced, realizing she'd revealed a little more than she'd planned. Unfortunately, Dallas had that effect on her. People found themselves telling their life story ten minutes after they met him. The man would have made a great psychiatrist or bartender. "Truth is, I didn't expect much from a town that willingly closed its own library so that Queen Rita could try her hand at yet another business."

"Ow!" He winced and held up a finger. "Give me a second." He slid his cell phone out of his back pocket and started typing away. After a few seconds, she decided to ask. "What *are* you doing?"

"What you forgot to do. Advertising. We need to get people to come by for a look-see with the possibility of a prize. Round up a box or something for people to put their entries into."

"What entries? I don't have a prize." While a prize might get some people to make a detour her way, it wasn't financially feasible. All business required some startup funds, but so far all she did was pay for stuff with nothing coming in. This soft opening wouldn't earn her any money and at best, she'd get some experience and learn what not to do at the next place. "Dallas. What kind of prize did you promise? A book?"

"A book might interest your readers, but many of them have to be driven here, so I said fifty dollars. That should interest the good folks of Emerson. I considered twenty-five, but that's not enough for a person to abandon their normal routine."

"Fifty dollars!" Both fists found purchase on her hips as she glared at Mr. Helpful. "You're fairly free with *my* money."

"Yeah, I am." He grinned and then laughed. "It's not your money." Dallas draped one arm over her shoulder as he said, "I'm putting up the fifty. I'm also playing up the possibility of something new in town. Everyone wants to be in the know, so they can be the expert the next day. Let's get things set up before the readers show."

Tenny sniffed. She wasn't comfortable with people doing things for her, but she knew Dallas meant well. "You're right."

A few minutes later she smoothed a tablecloth printed with a series of multicolored books across the table. She had a portable laminator to make library cards and a system set up on her laptop to track who checked out what book. At first, it might be a little unwieldy loading in addresses, but as long as she had phone numbers, she could let the borrower know if their book needed to be renewed or when the bookmobile would be in town next.

On her third trip back to the table with the brochures about bookmobile policies and upcoming events, she found Dallas squatting by a back tire and peering at it. "I don't like the looks of this one. I should have noticed this wear when we initially looked her over."

"Oh! That's the tire that got stuck in the pothole." She blew out a breath, ruffling her bangs as she recalled the dirt she choked down as the lever person. "It was no picnic getting the bookmobile out. I may have swallowed a gallon of dirty water, mud, and who knows what else." She shivered. "I'd rather not think about the last one."

Dallas grimaced at the recital. "Tenny," he drew out her name. "You should have called for help.

"Ha! Where we were, no one would have been able to find us. All the same, as a proud operator of a bookmobile, I must learn to manage on my own."

Not speaking, Dallas stood, crossed his arms, and gave the tire in question a small kick. "Okay," he conceded. "Miss Independence. You need a new tire, like, yesterday. You'll need it when this one goes. My feeling is it will be sooner than later."

"I'll put that on my to-do list." She made a mental note to do so, but lately, her ability to hold those unwritten reminders suffered some. A flattened hand shielded her eyes as she searched for a cow-spotted truck without any luck. It was so unlike Blue. She checked her phone for any texts about running late. Nothing.

Meanwhile, probably convinced he'd impressed the importance of vehicle safety on her, Dallas sat and returned to scrolling through social media notifications. He stopped as if aware of her stare.

"Your reading public is on its way. Might take them a bit. So…" His brows lifted as he glanced up at Tenny standing over him. "…what's this about your trying to track down whomever stole Rivertown's relocation money?"

Her hand slipped up to the back of her neck. *Darn.* "I should have known you'd hear that part of my ramble."

"It was kind of hard to miss."

His perceptive blue eyes caught hers—when he looked at her like that, it was as if he could see into Tenny's soul. If his pastor father had the same ability, parishioners probably ran to the altar, knowing their secrets had been found out. "Yeah, about that." A small red compact covered in bumper stickers headed their way, stopping her explanation. "I recognize that car from the car wash. We may have our first official bookmobile patron."

The vehicle stopped mere feet from them, close enough for Tenny to read a bumper sticker that asserted, *I'm not bossy. I just have better ideas than you.* Funny. A teenage girl with multicolored hair emerged and waved. "Did you get those anime books I suggested?"

"I did. You'll need to sign up for a card to check them out, though." She motioned her forward.

Dallas, who was at her shoulder, added in a whisper, "You might want to charge for the cards."

"That defeats the point of the library. It's supposed to be free, so all can use it." She smiled at her first visitor and slowly walked her through the library card sign-up. Before she knew it, another car showed, then some trucks, and a couple of SUVs. Doors slammed as readers and the curious headed their way. Dallas dealt with the contest entries, having people write their cell phone or landline numbers and names on sticky notes while chit-chatting with those he knew, which was everyone. He ended up doffing his straw cowboy hat, running both hands through his hair to eliminate obvious hat hair, and tossing the entries into the hat since no appropriate box had been found.

A good three dozen people signed up for library cards and all left with books. Maybe she was wrong about people not being interested in a library or a bookmobile. Another half-dozen people lingered at the table even after Tenny put up the closed sign. The men jingled change or keys in their pockets. One woman cleared her throat, but a little pig-tailed girl gave voice to their real purpose.

"Who won the money?"

Dallas grinned and picked up the hat. "I don't know. We haven't picked anyone yet. Would *you* like to pick the winner?"

"Yes!" The girl moved close to the table, shaping her right hand like a claw. Her mother offered instructions.

"Cindy, no need to dig deep. Plenty of entries right on top."

FROGS, FLOODS AND FRAUD

Dallas jostled the hat and then bent down, enabling the child to reach deep inside and pick out a folded piece of paper.

"What's it say?" Cindy asked.

"Moira Hopkins." Dallas read the name and a series of groans sounded. "I'm sure she'll be happy you drew her name. Good job!"

At times like this, Tenny almost wished she'd broken the most sacred of librarian vows and brought candy with her. Candy never had any place in a library because it made for sticky fingers, which resulted in sticky pages. "Here." She held out a bookmark with an image of the bookmobile on one side and contact information on the other. "Thank you for helping."

Cindy accepted the bookmark with delight. "I'm coming back as soon as I can read."

"Please do," Tenny encouraged with a smile. Normally, she'd mention to the parents how reading to their child helped them developmentally. Cindy's mother gave off the vibe of not being a bedtime story parent—then again, she could be wrong. On second thought, she added as she held up a brochure, "We'll be having special events with the bookmobile that you can keep track of online. Special children's programs that Cindy might like."

Cindy's mom took the offered brochure without a comment and herded her daughter toward a vehicle with a *Ask Me About Amway* banner across the windshield. As the last of the people moved toward their cars, Tenny pushed up her slipping glasses with one finger. "I lucked out with you helping. Blue was supposed to come by. I don't know what happened to her."

"I forgot to tell you she called me and asked me if I'd take her place."

"Oh." The elation she'd felt about his showing up dissipated.

He'd honored a favor, which explained his appearance. He'd probably climbed off his tractor or whatever a person did when they raised sunflowers as a crop.

Not noticing her mood change, Dallas continued, "Something about a dog named Moolah, a skunk, and some very unhappy cows. She may have said something about Griffin being upset, too."

"I can imagine. She has such a big heart when it comes to any living creature. Somehow, I ended up with a lame frog she rescued and named Fred. Currently, he's staying with the vet, who thinks it's a sprain as opposed to a broken limb. Fred should be swimming in the pond in no time."

"A frog with a pulled muscle. That sounds like Blue." A half smile crossed his face as he pushed a tendril of hair off Tenny's face. "You're pretty soft-hearted for babysitting a sick amphibian. Then there's the wrongly named Precious."

She suppressed a groan since the last thing she wanted to talk about was her mischievous raccoon and her complicated relationship with said creature. "Let's not talk about Precious."

"Okay. How about Rivertown's missing funds?"

Her eyelids fluttered open in irritation. Dallas was a thoughtful man, helpful to a fault, easy on the eyes—but he could *not* read the room. "Yeah, that's a long, twisted tale I'm having trouble figuring out."

"How about we grab dinner and you explain it to me?" he encouraged. "I can be useful figuring things out. Remember when your potato clock wouldn't work?"

His reference to her sixth-grade science project brought back the memory of her panicked state. Cinnamon had been unwilling to give up a plump potato for the project and gave her a withered one, assuming it would work just as well. It hadn't. Dallas, nearby with his plants and music trifold, had noticed her consternation. He sprinted off and returned with an oversized, fresh potato, which worked.

"You fixed it. I never asked you where you got the potato."

"Stole it from the lunchroom," he admitted with an eyebrow waggle.

"And you, a pastor's son, too."

"The next day, I brought in a five-pound bag of potatoes and left them in the kitchen. So," he lengthened the word, "it was more like borrowing. How about it? You..." He pointed to Tenny. "...and me." His thumb went back to himself. "If we put our heads together, we can probably solve half the problems of the world."

Just like that, her mood lifted again.

Chapter Twenty

TENNY PARKED HER bookmobile between the house and a grouping of oversized crepe myrtle where no one could complain about its presence since it would involve getting out of one's vehicle and walking up her driveway to catch a glimpse. Anyone doing so would be guilty of trespassing. The less friendly sorts around Emerson had metal signs with a pair of crossed guns on them in their windows, announcing trespassers would be shot. It was all show given that kids would cut through yards, a neighbor's cat might sun itself on numerous porch steps, and high school band members showed up as regular as the seasons, peddling oversized chocolate candy bars, with and without nuts. Making a fuss about someone in her yard would just be rude—just like a person complaining about her bookmobile. She walked backward, her hands tucked into her jeans back pockets, staring at her books-on-wheels vehicle, trying to gauge how visible it was.

Dallas waited in his idling pickup truck and powered the window down. "What are you doing?"

Noticing her neighbor, Belinda, she bypassed a shouted reply. Instead, she opened the passenger door and climbed inside. With the door closed and seatbelt secured, she twisted and gave her house a final glance. "The boxwood's getting fairly out of control. Uncle

Mark would have a fit if he were alive."

"Need help trimming it?" His hand went up in acknowledgment to the various neighbors who gawked from their porches. A few unabashedly moved into their front yards for a better look at who was driving the truck. A more charitable view would lean toward the neighbors being protective of the orphaned Tenny. More likely, they wanted to be accurate in their gossip.

After spending years in the city, her wave response time suffered. Occasionally, city folks greeted one another with a single finger. Tenny shot her hand up at the last minute to a shaggy-haired toddler on a big wheel trike. "No. Just the opposite. I like the boxwood that way. It helps hide the bookmobile."

"It will eventually scratch vehicles coming and going in your driveway."

"There is that." Why did he always point out the practical? She pursed her lips as she considered her options. "It's okay right now. I'll deal with it when it gets worse. As it is, no one can complain about my vehicle being an eyesore or my home not being zoned for a business."

"What?" Dallas' brow puckered and he mumbled something indecipherable.

"Couldn't hear you."

"That's the way I wanted it."

"Rude."

"Yep," Dallas agreed with a smile. "Besides, some things are best left unsaid in polite company."

"I'll give you that. Are you going to ask me what's got me so concerned about hiding my bookmobile?" she teased with a sideways look, knowing full well he would.

"Go ahead. Shoot."

"I got a call on my voice mail. Some woman trying to disguise her voice saying the bookmobile was an eyesore and my property wasn't zoned for business."

"Hmm…" Dallas murmured and stared straight ahead as he spoke. "If that were true, half the folks in Emerson would be in trouble."

"Exactly!" Tenny nodded with enthusiasm. "Besides, I don't conduct business at home. That's the last thing I want. People would hammer on my door at all hours because they'd discovered an overdue book."

"I hear you. Can't see how parking the bookmobile in your driveway is any worse than Joe Norwak parking his big rig in his drive."

"You're right!" Tenny sat up a little straighter, warming up to her subject, especially with a sympathetic listener. "What about all those oversized tractors, combines, and grain haulers? Huh!" She made a scoffing noise.

"Yeah, those. Any intelligent farmer keeps his equipment in a barn. They're not cheap and not easily seen from the road either. Your caller is just someone who wants to upset you. Can you think of anyone like that?"

She most definitely could. Instead of mentioning who, she changed the subject. "Where are we headed?"

"I thought we'd avoid the Almost Home Café. Not only would we be the conversational topic but everyone would be leaning so hard to hear what we were discussing they'd fall out of their seats."

The image of townspeople stopping in midbite of velvety carrot cake and listing to one side, eavesdropping, made her giggle. "It's good of you to care about the general populace."

"That's the kind of guy I am. Thought we'd grab a couple of Reubens from the new coffee and sandwich shop and eat them back at your house or my farm. The American Giant sunflowers are in full bloom. Some are up to fifteen feet. They're my last ones to bloom. It will be your only chance to see them before they're harvested. I've already cleared a couple of acres of the standard sunflowers."

"It's no contest. Your farm. At my place, we'll have Precious stealing our food. That reminds me, maybe we should pick up something for him."

Dallas slowed for a four-way stop and applied his brakes, swinging his gaze to Tenny as he carefully enunciated his words. "I'm *not* buying Precious anything."

After letting a flatbed truck stacked high with hay bales pass, he tapped the gas pedal and grumbled, "Sounds like you've fallen under that raccoon's spell. Like your aunt."

"I have not!" She held up her open palm as if to discourage any other remarks on the subject. Huffing slightly, she wiggled in her seat and managed a half pivot toward Dallas. "Precious doesn't need a spell. He tore my window screens when I wouldn't let him inside. He helps himself to anything edible and a few things not edible. Knocks things off the counter. Splashes water everywhere. He's more work to clean up after than a preschool class."

"And yet—"

"I don't talk about your toxic ex-wife, Rita, and you don't talk about Precious, and we'll have a good meal."

"Agreed!" Dallas shot out his right hand for a shake. Tenny pumped the offered digits and then released them.

At the sandwich shop, a silver Mercedes waited in the parking lot, pulling a groan from Tenny. What were the chances of running into her nemesis? Pretty good with the small populace and the town's entire restaurant offerings could be counted on one hand with a few fingers left over.

"No worries," Dallas remarked as he eased the car into a parking spot. "Too bad they don't have a drive-thru, but I hear they're working on it. I'll dash in and get our dinner. You can wait out here."

Even though the thought tempted her, it would be the coward's way. "No, I'll go in. I'll not let Rita influence what I can or can't do." Tenny grimaced. "That doesn't count as talking about Rita."

"Of course not." The crow's feet on his sun-kissed face increased as if he were trying to hide a smile. "Just to be fair, though. Precious! Precious! Precious!"

Tenny reached across the seat to poke him, but before she could, he wrapped his fingers around her wrist, stopping her for a moment. Their faces hovered inches apart. Dallas' blue eyes contained an indecipherable emotion, taking Tenny's breath away. The moment stretched wordlessly between the two of them until a loud gagging sound ruined everything.

Both Dallas and Tenny turned in time to witness Rita, elegantly turned out in a peach shift that flattered her blonde good looks, and her sidekick, the mousy Shadow, faring less well in a patchwork blouse that hinted at aging hippie, walking to the Mercedes while cradling oversized iced coffee concoctions. On cue, Shadow, who earned her nickname from existing in the more vibrant Rita's shadow, made the gagging noise again and announced loudly, "I saw something that turned my stomach!"

"Me, too," Rita agreed, pushing the fob on her keyring and re-ceiving an answering *beep*. "The tone of the place just took a nose dive."

A grim expression replaced Dallas' former indecipherable one, making it easy to guess his thoughts. He released his hold on Tenny's wrist, slid out of the truck, and slammed the door. He moved to the passenger door and assisted Tenny out. "Don't worry about those two. I think they are permanently stuck at age thirteen." He cocked his head as if considering the matter. "However, that's an insult to young teens. Let's say they're just stuck somewhere between troglodyte and bully."

Even though that sounded about right, Tenny tried for a smile as a reply. Just when she thought she could make it in Emerson with her bookmobile, creating friends as she went—not to mention Dallas—she'd always hit a huge speed bump named Rita. Back in the city, there may have been a student or staff member now and then who didn't like her. She never knew because being actual adults, they never mentioned it.

After grabbing their food and drinks, they headed to the farm. The setting sun dusted everything with a wide, gold-tipped paint-brush. The air remained relatively warm and, in the distance, goats bleated. Dallas parked the truck near a weathered picnic table.

The two of them exited, carrying their dinner, and sat at the table. Dallas brushed a few fallen leaves off the wooden surface. "It's not fancy. I could run inside and get a damp cloth."

He pressed his hands on the table to stand.

"Don't bother." Tenny unpacked her sandwich. "I don't intend to fully unwrap my sandwich. Peel as I go so, I don't lose any of the yummy ingredients."

"Good plan." Dallas resumed his seat and opened his sack. He passed over a bag of chips. "Tell me about your Rivertown issues?"

The man would ask when she had just taken a delicious bite of corned beef, melted Swiss cheese, and tangy sauerkraut on sturdy pumpernickel bread. She chewed determinedly while trying to convey information with her eyes.

"What's that?" Dallas cupped his ear, chuckling at his perceived wit and bit into his own sandwich. By this time, she washed down her food with some icy soda.

"I have to say I don't know much. Due to consistent flooding, the town got some money from various sources. They had it stored in a bank for relocation. Now, I'm not even sure how it was supposed to work—if they expected to all move together or what. Normally in the case of eminent domain, if your land is taken by the government for highways, airports, or other safety issues, a fair price must be paid for the land. What I don't get is, why wasn't each person paid for their land individually?"

"Could be they were getting ready to do that before the money vanished. Why Blue's cousin?"

Her lips pressed together as she considered the question. Several times she had asked herself the other side of that question—why not Jess? "She's the treasurer."

"Isn't that mainly a title?" He took a pull on his soda straw and continued, "Nowadays, money seldom touches hands. It's transferred into accounts. I doubt anyone handed Jess a bag full of money and told her to deposit it. Half the time, the bank doesn't even have the money you have in your own account. Just a little of it." He snorted. "That's why you're allowed to only withdraw so much at a time."

"Part of me knew this." Tenny blew out an audible breath and reached for her chip bag. "I guess I keep listening to rumors and, trust me, none of them are good. The money's gone, and Jess is, too."

Crunching chips, a few murmurs of satisfaction filled the air as the two polished off their dinner. A pair of blue jays engaged in a screeching match nearby, perhaps arguing who had rights over all the ripe sunflower seed. Dallas finished eating first, wadding up his wrappers and putting them back into the food sack. "So, *did* Jess vanish with the money?"

"The money vanished. I'm not even sure how long it had been gone when someone decided to check out the bank account, which had a zero balance. Fingers pointed at Jess since she was the treasurer. She was probably as shocked as the rest of them. She stayed around about a week and kept getting harassed in the process, and then she took off, which just made her look guilty."

"That would do it." Dallas drummed his fingertips on the table, resulting in Tenny's smirking.

"You always used to do that when you were thinking. It really irked some of the other students when we were doing group work."

The drumming stopped. "Did it bother you?"

"Just the opposite—it reassured me that I wasn't the only one working on the project. Like now."

"Good to know. What can you tell me about Jess?"

Tenny snorted. "Blue would be a better person to ask. All I know is she's only twenty and has been rather vocal about wanting to relocate. She collects celebrity autographs. Has done it a good part of her life. She has the signed photos framed and on her wall at home. I mention this because it feels odd that she didn't take those with her, even if her goal was to take the money and run. Left her cell phone, too."

"That's weird. I have a cousin that age and he carries his phone everywhere. When he helped me seed this spring, he stopped the tractor and went home because he forgot his phone. It wasn't as if he would spend the entire day helping me. It was just a couple of hours." Dallas shook his head in disbelief. "He *did* come back, but he wasted a good hour getting his phone. Told me he couldn't work without his playlist. What did Blue make of all this?"

Tenny rested her elbows on the table, interlaced her fingers, and rested her chin on them. "She accepted her aunt's story about people sending Jess nasty messages, and she abandoned her phone because of that. Aunt Hazel mentioned a new phone could be bought at any discount store."

"One that didn't come with all those harassing texts."

"My thoughts, too. That's basically what I know. I managed to find the names of everyone on the relocation board via the local paper. My plan was to follow the money to find out if anyone was spending money wildly. Your take?"

"Well…" He doffed his straw hat and placed it on the table. He ran his hands through his hair, explaining as he did so, "Sun is going down. No real reason for a hat. I'd be like those people who insist on wearing sunglasses inside."

"Go on," she urged, secretly glad he wasn't a hundred percent confident, demonstrated by his impromptu hairstyling. "Tell me your opinion."

"Whatever money is gone would be sizable. I'd expect the big guns to be looking into this, such as the FBI. The very fact that no one has handcuffed Jess and frog-marched her somewhere tells me there's no real evidence, just gossip. However, your idea of following the money is a good one. I also want to know who's fanning the finger-pointing at Jess. It would be the person with the most to gain. Rather like those magicians who trot out their assistants in their skimpy outfits, making all these unnecessary, showy dance moves to distract." His brows lowered and his frown deepened. "I happen to have personal experience with an expert in smearing innocent folks."

Tenny forced a laugh "No need to convince me. What if Jess *is* guilty? I hate to play the devil's advocate."

"Good thing Blue isn't here. I'd have to hold her back."

"I know." She sighed. "That's why I asked you. I could never ask her."

"Okay." He rubbed a bent knuckle between his brows. "She'd have to be the worst thief ever by forgetting to leave town the same time the money did. By this time, I imagine closed-circuit bank film has been examined. Money could have been moved a little at a time, which puts part of the burden on Jess for not noticing a diminishing account, but I'm sure she's not the only one with access to the account. I'm willing to bet the entire council could eyeball it."

That made sense. "I've served on my share of councils. We always had more than one person sign the check. Sometimes, it could be two people. In other cases, it was three. Maybe we have three dirty council members."

"Or one really good forger," Dallas inserted and covered her hand with his. "You can only do so much. Let the big guns do their job."

"Sounds like a plan." She audibly inhaled and added, "Blue's half convinced Jess has been abducted, despite the fact that the guy who runs the gas station saw her leave driving her own car."

"Big heart, even bigger emotions. Maybe it's a way to get people to feel sorry for her beleaguered cousin."

"No." Tenny's chin swung back and forth like a pendulum. "She believes it, mostly, and that her aunt isn't telling us everything."

"People seldom do." He turned over Tenny's hand and gently traced the lines on her palm. "What do you think?"

Hard to think with the sensation of his work-roughened fingers gliding over her palm. What had he asked her? Oh yeah, what did she think? "I try to remember what I was like at twenty. Even though I went away to school and maybe had toughened up a tad more than Jess, I still existed as a creature of mood swings and reactions. It wouldn't surprise me in the least if Jess decided she needed a break from everything and took off on a spa day or two."

Chapter Twenty-One

CONVERSATION FLOWED AS the sun dipped behind the sunflowers, sending up streamers of purple and red. Fresh-cut hay aroma floated in the air. The cicadas warmed up for their nightly concert, as did a few bullfrogs. Tenny blinked with surprise. Sunset already? Pointing to the direction where the frog quartet harmonizing came from, she asked, "Pond?"

Dallas gathered up the refuse on the table, combining it into one bag. "Just a stock pond really." He smirked as he continued. "The realtor told me it was a stocked pond. My assumption was bass, not frogs."

"Could be your frogs ate the fish, especially the juvenile ones."

"Never thought of that. I assume you'll be wanting to get home." He gestured back to the modest clapboard farmhouse. "Could I interest you in some television?"

Extending the night tempted until a yawn surprised her. She slapped a hand over her wide mouth and then giggled. "The spirit is willing, but the body is so tired. I noticed you don't have a dish."

"Now we get down to the real reason you turned me down," Dallas teased as he stood up and stretched.

"Oh, no. I kept the satellite dish and service that Uncle Mark initially bought. Both Aunt Cinnamon and I enjoyed watching old crime mysteries, often competing to see who could solve the case first. You'd be amazed how many times my aunt bested me."

"No, I wouldn't. Have you ever considered your aunt probably saw those shows the first time they ran, and possibly in reruns?"

A look of comprehension dawned on Tenny's face, accompanied by a snort. "That explains why she'd announce her suspicions at the beginning of the show after only watching eight minutes or so of the lead-in." Her shoulders went up into a shrug. "But it made her happy. What I was going to say is you're welcome to come over and watch a show or two with me. I might even scramble some eggs for both you and Precious."

The pleased expression on Dallas' face faded fast. "Not Precious. Think I'll pass."

"He just comes in to eat, and then he goes back outside. What do you have against raccoons anyhow?" His dislike bubbled up past the general trash panda nuisance factor. For the most part, Dallas kept an even keel about almost everyone and every animal. After all, she considered the man the ideal person to start an animal shelter, which reminded her of his earlier comment about having a few pets of his own. Outside of the cicadas, frogs, and quarrelsome blue jays, she hadn't seen hide nor hair of anything. As if on cue, a gray cat came around the corner of the house and meowed.

Dallas turned toward the cat and squatted, causing it to hurry in for a behind-the-ears scratch. "Theodora is here to rescue me from awkward questions."

"Not awkward. Just curious. I'll be the first to admit I'm not Precious' biggest fan, but you balk at the idea of coming over and watching television with me because of a raccoon?"

He scooped up Theodora and cuddled her against his chest as he spoke. "It's more than that. When we lived in Texas, I foolishly tried to assist a sick raccoon, and I ended up getting rabies shots. Not an experience I want to repeat."

"Did it have rabies?"

His lips pulled to one side. "No one knows. The ungrateful creature ran away. Still, I had the shots just to be safe, along with some other unpleasant treatments." He shuddered. "Not something I want to repeat."

"You'll be happy to hear Precious is up to date on his vaccinations. Doesn't that make you feel better?"

He carefully placed Theodora on the ground, straightened, cocked his head one way, then another, and shook his head. "Nope. I thought it would make a difference. It doesn't. Could take a while for me to get over my raccoon avoidance—if ever."

"Well, that doesn't bode well for a movie night with homemade pizza." It stung a little that spending time with her wasn't enough. As the son of a minister, he'd earned a reputation as an all-around nice guy. With both her aunt and uncle dead, her mother vanished decades ago, and her father unknown, she could be a soap opera character. He'd be nice. The question was, how nice? She shouldered her purse and headed for the truck.

"Wait!" Dallas lunged after Tenny, catching up by the virtue of his slightly longer legs. "You misunderstood me." He inhaled audibly before continuing. "I want to do things with you. C'mon, aren't we together now?"

"You're right," she grudgingly conceded. Still, sometimes, it felt like they only did what friends did—as opposed to an actual date. It could be she wanted more than he was willing to give. "It felt like you didn't want to go to my house."

"I picked you up, didn't I?"

"Technically, you followed me home and stayed in your truck as I parked the bookmobile. Not quite the same."

"All right." He whistled. "I've been told." He reached for her hand and entangled her fingers with his. "I'll admit I've tried to keep things balanced for a number of reasons. Right now, you've lost your family. It would be easy to cling onto someone without really feeling attracted."

Seriously? He went with that? Sure, she may not have been obvious in her affection for the teenaged Dallas, but she had tried by hanging out near his locker, saying hello every morning, and read all the Harry Potter books because it gave them something to talk about. She started the books for Dallas but kept reading for herself. "Is that all you got?"

They fell in step still holding hands, swinging them as they went. "Your neighbors would talk if I were seen going inside your house."

The possibility someone might talk about them made her chuckle. "They don't talk now?"

"Yeah, I see what you mean." He tugged on her hand, pulling her in a different direction. "I need to close the chicken coop door before we go."

"You have chickens?" Lots of people owned chickens in the country—why not Dallas?

"That might explain the coop. With Beau, my dog, visiting with little Jeff next door, I can't take a chance on losing chickens. Plenty of animals enjoy a chicken dinner, such as coyotes, foxes, and even weasels. Beau's presence might discourage some, but if any of the hens decide to take a midnight stroll, they could be picked off by an owl."

A red pre-fabricated chicken coop resembled a single-room schoolhouse, complete with a bell tower minus a bell. "You want to go inside?"

"I'm good waiting here." Tenny was not certain about chickens since her aunt and uncle raised her as a town person as opposed to a farm girl. The only way chickens figured into her life was at mealtime and once a year at the 4-H Fair.

Dallas dropped her hand and slipped inside the wire fence. Even though a low clucking resonated, no poultry patrolled the yard. A ramp led up to a small opening, similar to a dog door. There was a people-sized door cut into the coop, too. Dallas stuck his head into the people door and said a few words, which increased the clucking. Even the chickens loved him, or they could be complaining about their days. After securing the big door, he bent and secured the smaller one. He wiped his hands on his jeans and then exited the coop. "The girls are up. Normally, they head for the coop when the sun sets or earlier. People call chickens stupid, but they do understand safety."

They fell into step as they headed to his truck. "Where's your dog again? Visiting?"

"Yeah." He cleared his throat. "The neighbor kid, Jeff, actually owned Beau's sister, She-Hulk."

"She-Hulk, huh?"

"He's eight. The kid couldn't come up with a dignified name like Beauregard Fluffy Butt."

"You don't call your dog that!"

"I only resort to the full name when he's in big trouble, which is almost never. Anyhow, She-Hulk vanished. We thought having Beau around might bring home the missing dog faster, especially since they're relatives." He nudged Tenny. "Maybe you could concentrate on She-Hulk as opposed to Rivertown's missing funds."

"I'll consider it when I'm done with Rivertown, which, with any luck, will be soon."

They strolled to the passenger side. Dallas swung the door open and waited for Tenny to settle before closing it. She blew out a breath. Best to move on to something else equally provocative.

The seats creaked as Dallas swung into place behind the driver's wheel. Before he could say a word, Tenny ambushed him. "I'm okay with being friends. I like to think we were always friends, and I'd like to continue it. No reason for you to make up any more obviously fake excuses to be otherwise."

"All right." He started the engine and the dashboard lights illuminated the cab before the overhead dome light faded. Although brief, it allowed her a visual of his set chin and furrowed brow.

"What's wrong?"

"I worry about you."

"Hey, I'm a big girl."

"Not denying you're capable. Still, you're a nice person and you expect others to play by the rules. Trust me, I know. I got sucked in by a manipulative non-rule player. Almost chewed off my arm in the process to get away. While I want to see you, I worry how much trouble I'm stirring up for you."

"You mean by the person who shall not be named."

"Yeah, her."

"She's a spoiled brat who gets everything she's ever wanted."

"Well…" Dallas hesitated and blew out a breath. "…maybe everything was fine, at least from her point of view, when she got what she thought wanted. Rita never accepted I had the nerve to divorce her. She tells everyone it was her. She also says no one in this town is good enough for her. I think most of the men learned from my experience. As far as her company, no one wants to do business with her. Insuring your crop is a way to make it through the year sometimes. Why would any farmer go with someone with a track record of quitting everything she starts? When a crop fails, she'd be off to another venture."

"You're not telling me anything I didn't know—except for no one using her agency. No big surprise there. Still," her hand slipped up to rub her neck, "how does any of it have anything to do with me?"

"Yeah, that." He flicked on the headlights and pointed the truck toward the main road. "Rita has never taken responsibility for her own actions. She blames others when things don't go her way. You're her latest target."

She held up an index finger and said matter-of-factly. "That, I knew."

"What you probably don't know is that she can be dangerous when she doesn't get her way."

"Rumors flew when the widow who owned the prize winning palomino filly refused to sell to her."

"Yeah, that." His lips tightened and he shrugged his shoulders. "That accident of the widow falling into the well did make a person wonder. The filly had already been sold by that time, though. Obviously, the widow saw through Rita and knew she was no animal lover. The widow's death was ruled accidental."

It had struck Tenny odd at the time that a woman who'd lived on the farm most of her life forgot the location of the well. "Most believed otherwise. Often the police don't pursue cases when they don't have enough evidence—doesn't mean they don't think it could have been homicide."

Dallas grunted in reply and added, "That's why it may seem like I'm blowing hot and cold, but I don't want Rita after you any more than she already is."

"On that point, we agree. Besides, how much worse can she do than she already has?"

Chapter Twenty-Two

A BRIGHT TRILL of robin-song filled the dark. "Stupid birds. Why can't they sleep like everyone else?" Tenny muttered, dragging her pillow over her face. Familiar with the various nocturnal birds and their songs, she groaned when she heard a bright cardinal chirping. "They're not a night bird." She wiggled her way across the mattress to the glowing bedside clock. The red numerals read 4:45 a.m. Technically morning, but not by her standards. The cardinal-song flowed into golden finch notes. Mockingbird. Of course. She should have known. According to a book she'd read on birds, a mockingbird imitates other birds, creating an illusion of a crowded area and forcing potential nesters to look elsewhere. She flopped over to her back and stared at the ceiling, just barely making out the light fixture.

Normally, she tried to sleep until six. Her lips twisted as she tried to imagine falling back to sleep with the bird version of the Mormon Tabernacle Choir mere feet from her head. Nope, not happening. Her bare feet hit the rug while she searched with her left hand for her glasses. Finding the needed lenses, she plopped them onto her face and blinked, trying to bring things into focus without much success. "Oh yeah." She snapped on the bedside lamp, improving her vision immeasurably.

Tenny shuffled to the kitchen, trying to remember her plan for the day as she poured water into the coffee maker. Blue called last night and asked about revisiting Rivertown after she and Griffin completed the first milking. Despite all her brave talk about locating Rivertown's missing funds by following the money, she liked Dallas' suggestion about letting the big guns handle any financial shenanigans. So far, she'd witnessed nothing—not a single government employee in sight driving an unremarkable sedan and dressed in inconspicuous clothes so as to not stand out. In Rivertown, an FBI agent who hoped not to attract notice would don overalls or hip waders with a favorite fishing hat. Wearing all three would cinch it.

At least she had the names of the council members. Blue found their home addresses as opposed to post office boxes. It sure would be nice to drive by and see a sparkling new Mastercraft fishing boat attached to a matching F-250 truck. Surely people didn't drop that kind of money every day. Smart criminals, which television loved to portray since they could keep them returning for follow-up episodes, wouldn't spend any money. They'd either sit on it for a decade or get it to another country where they could spend it without too much notice.

After the coffee finished brewing, Tenny poured herself a cup, sat down, and tried to remember what Dallas had said previously about banks and money seldom touching hands. The Federal Deposit Insurance Corporation insured each depositor for up to $250,000, if they had that much. Would they pay out on the missing money? Would they consider it one depositor or several?

A memory of a movie, or was it a book, lodged in the back of her mind—something about banks and missing funds. Maybe more coffee would cause the memory half hiding in her brain to step out of the shadows.

An hour later, she'd served Precious breakfast, dressed, and poured herself some cereal and was just about ready to drown it in milk when a knock sounded. Not waiting for a little thing like someone actually answering the door, Blue sauntered in garbed in a Moo Town black-and-white Holstein spotted hat and a matching shirt topping her ripped jeans.

"Hey, girl! You're getting crazy, leaving your door unlocked and all."

"Yeah." She crinkled her nose. "Look what happened when I failed to relock the door after letting Precious in. Some crazy chick garbed in spotted cow clothes barges in. What next?" She threw up her hands, feigning astonishment.

"Ha!" Blue crossed her arms and smirked. "Here I was going to do something nice for you, but I'm not so sure now."

"Hmm…" Tenny played along, well aware her friend wasn't the type to offer something, then yank it away. "What gift might that be?" Her eyebrows lifted with the question.

She popped up one finger and gave a backward glance over her shoulder. "No gift. A treat. We need to get going."

Curious about her friend's backward glance, she moved closer to a window and spied Moolah tied to lawn furniture and currently shredding a potted plant. "Ah, I see you brought your dog."

"Yep. I'm interested in that training Marvin promised me." She placed one hand on her hip and cleared her throat. "Griffin insists that Moo must learn manners or find a new home."

Any thinking person would say the same thing, but how Blue took it would be something else entirely. Tenny sat, poured her milk, picked up her spoon and said, "You're going to do whatever Griffin tells you?"

"Normally, no." Blue dropped her casual pose, glanced out the window again and made a clucking sound with her tongue. "I'm sorry about your plant."

"No worries. The year's winding down and the plants are dying off." Not necessarily that particular plant, though, which had more than a few weeks of life in it. Still, there was no reason to mention it and make her friend feel bad. "Go on," she gestured with her hand.

Blue sighed, pacing with her hands behind her back. "I know I'm a lucky woman. My husband bends over backward to make me happy. He watches all those rom-com movies he hates so much with me. He drove me to Chicago for my birthday, so we could see that boy band you and I loved so much."

"Back Alley Boys." Tenny spooned cereal into her mouth, chewed, and then continued, "He must love you. I can't name any husband who would do the same."

"He's a good one." She rubbed an open hand over her face, knocking her hat askew. "And he's not wrong about Moolah. Our girls have been bellowing more than usual and engaging in head-butting and kicking behavior, which we seldom see. It's Moo. I do my best to keep him away from the cows." She gave a slow head wag. "It doesn't do any good. He's an escape artist. Before I know it, he's out of the house, barking up a storm and nipping at the girls' hooves. Milk production was down significantly this morning."

Using her empty spoon to point at Blue, she said, "That's a real problem."

"Tell me about it! We have to get him to the dog whisperer and hope Rita doesn't drop in again."

"Maybe." Tenny tucked a tendril behind her ear. "Marvin might have one of those programs where you leave your dog for two weeks and he comes back as a well-behaved dog."

"Wonderful." Blue clapped her hands together. "Let's ask. Hurry up and eat. Moo might be moving onto the lawn chairs with his destruction campaign."

Dribbling a little milk in the process, Tenny wolfed down her cereal and allowed the spoon to clatter into the empty bowl. "I need to get Precious outside. I'm supposed to pick up Fred today, too, which means we need to get back before the vet closes. Who knows? He may be swimming with his buds before the week is out."

Blue knocked the heel of her hand against her forehead. Her cap fluttered to the floor. "I even forgot about Fred!" Her mouth dropped open followed by a huff. "Moolah is a full-time dog and then some. The sooner we get to the Canine Stampede, the easier my life will be."

There was no reason to mention Marvin's much-championed dog training skills could simply be a sales pitch. "I'm pretty sure he'll expect you to pay this time."

"I'm more than willing to do so."

"All right, then." Tenny snapped her fingers for Precious. No results. Not that she truly expected him to come running. Maybe Marvin might branch out to wildlife, but she doubted it. She might as well go with one of the tried and true methods. Sure, he exited nicely the other night, but that was a fluke. She reached into the cupboard, pulled out a box of cookies, and shook them. A masked face peered into the kitchen. Seeing him, Tenny rattled the box again. "We're eating outside. Let's go." She motioned to the back door and got both Blue and Precious moving in that direction.

Precious moved down the concrete steps at an angle, taking tiny steps and keeping Tenny and the cookie box in sight. In doing so, he totally missed the out-of-control canine anchored to the wooden Adirondack chair. However, Moolah didn't miss Precious and let out an ear-splitting bay and lunged, dragging the chair across the concrete patio.

"Oh no!" Tenny gasped as she watched in slow motion the leg of the chair pull away from the frame—the same chair she'd helped her uncle make.

Blue leapt from the stairs, bypassing the last two steps, and then snapped up the leash at the same time as the chair leg broke. "Moolah! Look what you did!" She turned toward Tenny. "I'm so sorry about your chair."

She was, too—sorry, that is. Staring at the busted chair, she found herself wordless. Did the chair represent her life? Listing to one side and not very useful? It made her wonder. Back at the university library, she actually served a purpose. Noticing her friend's glassy eyes, she tried for a joke. "I didn't need three chairs anyhow. So, where's this treat you promised me?"

Precious scampered out of view without even a cookie, possibly afraid he'd get blamed for the chair but probably more dog shy. With the leash wrapped around her hand a couple of times, Blue gave it a yank. "I'm driving! That's your treat. The truck has high suspension and four-wheel drive, which means we shouldn't get stuck anywhere."

It would also save wear and tear on the bookmobile, especially the carpet. With Blue sure of her destination, this trip should go much faster, except for Moolah. "I'm not holding Moolah, am I?"

Blue chuckled as she headed for the driveway. "No. I brought a crate for him. Can't have him all over the truck now, can I?"

"No, you can't," she started, and then stopped. Her lips pressed together, and she sniffed. "Where was the crate when he piddled in the bookmobile?"

"Griffin borrowed it from the Johnson farm. They used it until they trained their dog well enough that he could be trusted outside the crate. I plan to do the same with Moolah."

Tenny glanced at the dog and whispered, "Looks like you're going to be in that crate a long, long time."

"I heard that!" Blue declared with a touch of indignation. "You'll be amazed how different he'll be by this afternoon. It'll be as if I'm bringing home a totally different dog."

Tenny pressed a hand to her heart. "I'm more than ready to be awed. I have some theories I want to run past you on the way there."

Chapter Twenty-Three

D UE TO THE wetness of the ground, harvesting would have to be put on the back burner as farmers waited for a stretch of sunny days to dry out the crop. Farmers drifted into town, hanging out at the feed and seed store, the hardware store, or treating themselves to coffee and a grumble at the local diner. School buses buzzed by, carrying students who'd rather spend the Indian Summer day outside as opposed to inside a building. As for Tenny and Blue, the pet crate war had just started.

To say Moolah objected to the crate would be an understatement. Tenny and Blue wrestled the resistant dog into the crate while a neighboring child took it upon herself to assist by giving instructions. After constant barking left her ears ringing, Tenny asked her, "What did you say?"

The pony-tailed girl stuck her chin up in the air and huffed before speaking, "I don't think she likes the crate."

"She's a he," Blue corrected. "I just think he needs to get used to it. Tenny, give Moo a cookie."

Cookies failed to meet the nutritional requirements of canines. They weren't all that great for people either, come to think of it. She shoved a cookie through the crate bars and it disappeared into Moo's mouth. Their unasked-for supervisor loudly cleared her throat. "Where's my cookie? I helped, too!"

Tenny held out the open box, into which their helper stuck both hands and pulled out fistfuls of bite-size cookies. She skipped away, possibly scouting out a place to hide while consuming her chocolate chip haul without sharing.

The truck door slammed on the side of the double cab where Moo resided. Blue headed to the driver's side. It was road trip time—only this time, Tenny expected much better results. Using her flattened hand as a shield for her eyes, she stared up at the blue sky. There wasn't a cloud in sight, which should mean no showers. The thought lightened her mood. As she climbed into the truck, she remembered the old saying about Indiana weather—it could change in a minute. You could have snow, hail, rain, and sunshine all on the same day.

The engine growled to life and Blue reversed down the drive. Tenny held her comments as they waved to various folks out and about before asking the most pertinent question. "Anything else from Jess?"

"Nothing," Blue mumbled, staring straight ahead.

Talk about a non-answer. Normally, Blue would half turn to reply, making Tenny nervous if her friend happened to be driving. Today, she failed to meet her eyes. Something was up. Being the other member of the mystery-solving team, she needed info.

"I know…" Tenny began easing into her subject. "…that with a person as old as Jess, the police don't do a whole lot. They usually call it a runaway. And Jess may have more reason to run away than most." Her brow puckered as she considered a mitigating factor. "Ah, most of my information has come from television shows and podcasts. I never have known a missing person in real life. Did your aunt notify the authorities?"

"Nope."

"You're full of one-word answers today. Did you call your aunt and ask her directly if she reported Jess missing?"

On this note, Blue turned and gave her a long stare.

"Well then," Tenny stalled, surprised to get such a look from her friend but then continued, "your aunt chose not to notify the authorities of Jess' disappearance. When we were there, she acted much more interested in picking a new town than searching for her daughter, treating her more like a stray cat, in a *she'll come home when she's hungry* manner."

"Yep."

"Enough! You know something and you're not sharing. I thought we were a team."

Blue released an audible breath. "I'm not sure if I should. It could make you an accessory."

That sounded ominous. Had her friend suddenly capitulated to her side of the where-did-the-money-go equation? However, she doubted her theory when Dallas helpfully pointed out that banks seldom had the physical money that the account showed. They merely existed as numbers, which explained why anyone who wanted to draw out a large sum of money couldn't do it all at once or had to wait to do so.

Scraggy pines, a few redbud trees, and a stand of birch flew by outside her window, along with cows standing in a field. She wondered if Blue would say anything—silence would make it a more awkward trip. The snores signaled that at least Moo had calmed down. Thankfully, Blue remained awake.

"Aunt Hazel *knows* where Jess is."

The words delivered quietly surprised Tenny, who had wondered about the very thing. "Did she say she knew where she was?"

"No."

"Do you think Hazel knows where Jess is?"

"I know she does." She gave an emphatic nod, and then turned to Tenny.

"Eyes on the road," Tenny reminded. "I'm in the cab and can hear just fine without your turning."

Blue giggled. "I keep forgetting how uptight you are about driving."

"Not uptight. Cautious. Your aunt is lying?"

"Pretty much," Blue answered, keeping her eyes on the road. "You know the women in my family can't keep a secret."

"You did tell me about my surprise twelfth birthday party."

"Sorry about that. Anyhow, I asked my aunt if she contacted the authorities and she said there was no need. When I asked why there was no need, she pretended it was a bad connection and hung up. I didn't want to tell you. What if the police talked to us or the FBI? We would be withholding information. What would be the penalty for that?"

"If it's a felony, you can be fined up to two hundred and fifty thousand dollars and possible imprisonment for three years." Her nose crinkled as she added, "We had a lot of pre-law students in the university library. As a reference librarian, I constantly answered questions about sentencing for various crimes—stuff they should have known or looked up on their own."

Blue sucked in her lips and muttered, "Who will help with the milking if I'm in prison?"

"You don't know anything. All you know is your aunt has a

secret. Actually, her secret could be she dyes her hair."

"Everyone knows that. No way that color is natural."

Tenny's lips tipped up, finding amusement in the situation. "What I'm saying is, you know nothing of merit. Lots of people lie every day about silly things. It doesn't mean they're part of a criminal coverup. Maybe your aunt does know where Jess is. Maybe she jumped on the back of a Harley and decided to be a biker babe."

"Not Jess." Blue's voice grew stronger and more certain. "An accident on a motorbike when she was twelve had her swearing off two-wheelers."

"Okay." Tenny held her hand up. "That was an example. It could be something your aunt doesn't want spreading all over town. It could be embarrassing."

"More embarrassing than Jess' robbing the town?"

"Put that way, it would have to be bad. What did Jess' text say again?"

Blue held one finger up. "I'm thinking. Umm, it was, I need to tell you something."

"So, no help? No, I'm being abducted? Or, call the police?"

"Nope."

"I did think you acted fairly cool today. The other day you were certain ransom demands would be forthcoming."

"Yeah, that." She managed a weak laugh. "Griffin explained how irrational my fears were. I wanted to believe in a kidnapping because it somehow seemed better than my little cousin's being a thief."

A silver Mercedes zoomed passed them on the left, blaring its horn as it did so. Tenny stated the obvious. "Rita. I wonder what mayhem she's in the process of creating."

"Better off not knowing. We don't want to be accessories," Blue mentioned with a grin.

"Oh c'mon! You know we both would turn her in in a heart-beat." Even though Aunt Cinnamon claimed Tenny didn't have a mean-spirited bone in her body, she'd beg to differ when it came to Rita. "We'd search for a public phone, and then make an anonymous tipster call."

"That's an idea." Blue slapped the steering wheel with one hand. "Let's do it. I know she's up to something."

"No." Even though a smile at the prospect still graced her face, Tenny shook her head. "In Indiana, reporting false information about a crime is a misdemeanor, punishable by a year in prison. This one I know by heart. It made me wonder what those pre-law students were up to."

"Geesh," she moaned. "You're no fun. Way to ruin a plan with cold, hard facts."

"Trying to keep you on the right side of the law. Her nose crinkled at the thought of Blue in jail. "No one would believe you'd do something so underhanded, so you'd probably get away with it, but Rita would know."

Blue shivered. "I wonder if young Emerson mothers warn their children about the dangers of getting on the wrong side of Rita."

"If they don't, they should." Tenny's glib comment brought back Dallas' warning about his ex-wife. "Do you think we should worry about Rita? I mean, do you think she's dangerous as opposed to just being super annoying?"

"I don't know." Blue drove a little longer before continuing her thought. "Rumor is, Rita's on the hunt for a sugar daddy. Turns out her parents might not be as flush as they once were. Cryptocurrency investments—they sunk a bundle into the new currency. Apparently, they couldn't read the signs and lost everything—close to a half million."

Tenny whistled at the amount. "Gotta love small towns where no secret stays secret for long."

Chapter Twenty-Four

U NLIKE THEIR PREVIOUS Rivertown trip, things went better than expected. Blue sang along with her favorite Back Alley Boys songs with Tenny joining in on the chorus. Sir Moolah somehow slept through it. The sun shone, traffic remained light, and they couldn't ask for much more. With everything working in their favor, they made it to Canine Stampede in record time.

A half-dozen dogs romped together in the outside fenced area, giving evidence of improved business. After parking and waking Sir Moolah, Blue and Tenny entered the lobby where they tripped a motion alarm that barked. Marvin came out of a back room, drying his hands. "Welcome to Canine Stampede! Where your dog is king…" He swung into his usual spiral without even glancing to see who had entered. His expression changed when he recognized his visitors. A huge grin threatened to take over the bottom half of his face. "Well, I'll be. You came back!"

Blue stepped forward, pulling on the leash, but rather than go with her, Sir Moolah sat and gave a few sharp barks—possibly giving his opinion on the matter. "You promised to train my pup and I'm willing to pay. Hopefully, you won't get a particular visitor that will prevent that from happening. What's your normal training price?"

"Well now, I haven't given that much thought." He hooked his thumbs under each side of the bib on his overalls. "You're the first one to ask."

Tenny gestured to the outside area. "What about all the dogs in the yard?"

"Not much money being made there." He snorted and ran his hand over his bald pate. "I guess I thought there was more of a call for a dog kennel and daycare than there seems to be."

"It takes a while for people to notice," Tenny assured while remembering some folks in Emerson didn't even know they had a library until it was closed. "Have you done any advertising?"

"You mean besides walking around town? It did get me one customer."

They all shared a laugh with the exception of Sir Moolah, who stared back at the door longingly. A rustle of a dog treat box being opened drew the reluctant dog's attention. Acting unaware of Moolah's sudden interest, Marvin continued speaking while moving the small bone-shaped treat in his hand. "I put up some flyers in the local stores, which netted me the six customers' dogs outside. However, they're on their first free visit. The real question is, will they come back? Not sure how I'll ever pay off my loan at this rate. It cost plenty to build this place. The land didn't come cheap either. I didn't think any bank would approve my business plan, but my son, Lloyd, works at a bank." He raised his chin and pushed his shoulders back as he continued. "He told me not to worry since his bank would fund it. I didn't have to put a penny down. Very helpful since I'd already spent all I had buying the property."

Odd. Tenny pursed her lips as she considered how Lloyd helped his father get a loan. Most people might think banks give out money willy-nilly, but that had never been her experience. When her uncle

Mark wanted to expand his hardware business by opening another store in Beechnut, he got turned down. The loan officer decided Beechnut couldn't support two hardware stores. Disheartened, her uncle never tried another bank. Nowadays, Beechnut had three or more hardware stores. Tenny abandoned her walk down resentful lane when she witnessed the troublesome pup sitting up for a treat as if he'd done it all his life.

This pleased Marvin, possibly more than Blue. "Will you look at that? I think your little buddy already knows a few tricks. He just needs some polishing up."

"Wonderful!" Blue chirped, pressing her hands together. "How about twenty an hour? We should be gone just a couple of hours. How much do you think you can teach him in that time?"

Marvin picked up Moolah and tucked him under one arm and bunched the leash in his hand. His nose crinkled as he explained. "It doesn't work exactly that way. I won't do more than an hour of training at the most. Dogs are like kids. They get bored easily. Once I lose his attention, I might as well quit."

Half listening to the conversation, Tenny wondered why Marvin had got a loan when her uncle Mark hadn't. "Is your son the loan officer?"

Realizing she had vocalized her thoughts, Tenny slapped both hands over her mouth. Blue shot her a speculative glance that promised more questions later. Rather than being appalled at her nosiness, Marvin shook a finger at her. "You're not after my son, are you? Or possibly a loan?"

"Absolutely not," a red-faced Tenny declared. "Forget I said anything. I must have been thinking about a show I watched on television."

"Uh-huh." Marvin allowed his disbelief to sound in the two syllables. He shrugged. "You could do worse. Unlike me, he still has all his hair. Takes after his mother. He's not the loan officer, but he does something with computers. The heart of the bank, actually. He's on call all the time. I like you, Tenny. You strike me as an honest, hardworking gal. Lloyd would do well to step into a double harness with someone like you." He made a face. "You're so normal. Not like your fancy friend who wasted my time the other day."

Both Blue and Tenny replied in unison. "She's not our friend."

"Yeah." Marvin's eyes crinkled with amusement." I'd say you two have some strong feelings on the matter. Get going. The sooner you leave, the sooner you get back."

They agreed and promised to be back soon. Blue made kissy noises in an effort to attract her dog's gaze. The pup cuddled into Marvin's chest, changing loyalties as easily as most people change socks.

By the time the truck door closed, Blue swung into full-scale grumble. "Did you see Moolah ignore me for Marvin?"

"Yes, I saw that."

"After everything I've done for him!" She shoved the key into the ignition and twisted it.

"You know, his previous owner could be an older man like Marvin. What if he wasn't on his own, but exploring, as some dogs do?"

Blue huffed a reply and put the truck into drive. They left the parking lot with a spritely honk, and then hit the main road. After a few miles, Blue cut her eyes to her friend. "Griffin suggested the same thing. I'm always on this mission to save animals, and a few select people believe, such as you and Griffin, that I never stop to consider if the animals even wanted help." Her lips pulled down into a mulish expression for a few seconds, and then she asked, "What if someone is missing their adorable pup?"

He was not exactly adorable, but someone could miss him all the same. "Don't they have some type of Petfinder site online? You could check and see if anyone's posted a description that sounds like Moolah."

Blue blew out an exasperated breath. "I suppose I should. It's the only decent thing to do. I'll check once I get home. Better yet, I'll tell Griffin and he'll look it up immediately. He'd put up found dog."

"Don't think he'd go that far." However, the image of Griffin running into the house and booting up the computer to find Moolah's former owner sounded about right. "In the end, you want him to be with his real family."

"I suppose so." Blue tapped a notebook resting underneath the emergency brake handle. "I have the addresses of the council members in there. Remember what you said about following the money? We take a simple drive and see who has what?"

"That's one way," Tenny half-heartedly agreed. Her hand went up to tuck an escaping ginger curl behind her ear. "On crime dramas, forensic accountants are able to trace money trails mainly using bank records."

"What's up with your question about Marvin's son being a loan officer? Rude. It implied his business wasn't a good bet."

Her aunt would roll in her grave if she thought Tenny had showed bad manners. Aunt Cinnamon emphasized family, kindness, manners and literacy. After family, it was hard to say which one tied for second place. "I didn't mean it that way. Business loans are some of the hardest to get. People buying houses and cars, even with so-so credit, still get loans. Maybe their interest rates are higher than they might like. Uncle Mark could never get a loan for a new store. He wanted a branch in Beechnut, but he could have expanded his store in Emerson, too."

"I hear you. As you know, we'd love to expand our milking barns, but we need to come up with a huge chunk of money on our own before even asking for a loan. On one hand, you have a point. Still, it was rude."

"I know. Wish I'd kept my mouth shut. Then, he had to compliment me by calling me honest and hardworking. I might as well be a Boy Scout."

"No worries. I'm sure you're not interested in Lloyd."

"You're right. I guess I would rather sound a little more alluring than a truthful draft horse."

"Forget about it. Pick up the book and read me the first address."

Tenny flipped the book open. "Margie Fleenor, 42 Frank Ott Road."

"I think I know where that is. Jess and I rode horses up that road when we were younger. Watch for the cross-street signs. They're not big, and usually, you don't notice them until you pass right by."

"Great street planning." She pushed her glasses up and leaned forward as if the extra couple of inches would allow her better observation skills. A worn sign showed up ahead, but the sun-faded letters could have been anything. "Slow down. I can tell there are three words there, but I can't read them."

The speed dropped and on the right side, a large apple sign promised *The Best Little Apple Orchard* was up the road. Blue flipped on her blinker and turned.

"You don't even know if this is the right road."

"Sure, I do. The Best Little Apple Orchard is on Frank Ott Road." She delivered the words as if everyone in the world knew this informational tidbit. "It's a very small town. There are only so many roads."

"I figured as much. Drive slowly so I can read the house numbers. Do we know anything about Margie?" Television detectives quickly ferreted out who needed money, gambled excessively, or was open to bribery. She twisted in her seat, watching rows of apple trees marching into the distance in somewhat uniform lines.

"I called my aunt. Despite what she said about not talking to anyone in town since they had the bad taste of thinking Jess might have helped herself to the funds, she still is. Good for us since it keeps us apprised of the local gossip. Let me see if I can remember what she said about Margie."

The truck topped the hill and a trio of dogs left their perch on a mobile home deck and chased after them, fading fast as the truck kept moving. To the right, a neat little farm with a red barn and silo came into view. As they moved closer, an older couple packed boxes into a brand-new fifth wheel camper hooked up to a Ford F-450 truck. A pair of binoculars would have helped to check out the name on the massive camper and do a price check later. "I think we may have some lavish spending here."

Blue barely glanced at the couple bustling around like busy ants ready to flee the anthill for life on the open road. It might make them much harder to track, too. Shocked her friend didn't even give the obvious evidence a second glance, she nudged Blue. "Did you see that huge camper? That must have cost a bundle, and what about the truck? Those dually trucks don't come cheap."

"I saw it," Blue confirmed. "Griffin and I attended one of those

Home and RV shows. Some of the super nice gooseneck trailers go for over a hundred thousand."

"My point. What about Margie as our thief? Aren't you going to turn around and look at least?"

Blue's shoulders went up into a shrug, and she stifled a yawn before replying, "I know all about the camper. They ordered it almost two years ago. The couple planned on hitting the road when Margie's husband retired. They paid for the camper a while back. It took so long to actually get it—something to do with the inability to get components. No new money spent there. The entire town has heard about their plan to drive across the United States a few dozen times by now."

The ballpoint pen nib hovered over the name. Instead of crossing it out, Tenny pulled the pen back. "What if they did order the camper, which everyone knew about, but decided a little extra money would make the trip across the states so much easier? No one would be suspicious of them when they left. Seemed to me as if they were rushing."

"They were. They want to get their campsite while the weather holds." Blue doffed her hat and fluffed her hair, peering into the mirror as she did so. The truck swerved a bit, but Blue corrected it. "You suspect everyone."

"That's the nature of an investigation. Everyone is a suspect until they aren't." So far, every council member was a suspect. It could also be possible a non-council member served as the culprit, but who would have access to the funds?

Chapter Twenty-Five

NEWS OF A black-and-white spotted truck creeping along Rivertown's roads hit the gossip hotlines fast. According to Blue's aunt, if they made the bad decision to pull into someone's driveway, the business end of a shotgun might greet them. Not sure why Blue would do such a thing. Their initial goal of eyeballing everything from a safe distance yielded no results. Lavish spendings, such as an Italian sportscar, a fishing boat with oversized engines, or even an expensive racehorse couldn't be found. Then again, only the foolish would broadcast a financial windfall, especially when no legitimate explanation for it existed. In small towns, everyone knew if your relative died and who inherited what. All the same, they had to try if only for Jess' sake.

Aunt Hazel remained on speaker phone as Tenny read the names. "Council member Jeff Jones. What can you tell me about him?"

"He used to run a barber shop and auto parts store."

"Unusual combination."

"Not really. It worked out well. A guy could get a part for his tractor and a close shave with one stop." She took an audible sip before continuing, "You know, with people leaving left and right, he shuttered his businesses just about the time the twins were at the start of their senior year."

"Graduating children?" Tenny surmised. "Two of them, too. I bet he could use some money for college or trade school tuition."

"Probably could if he still had a business. With Jeff losing his business and the town forced to move, it pushed Donnie and Danny into contenders for full state scholarships. Both boys are good students. If our county had a bigger school, the baseball team might have taken state honors with Danny on the mound. He's that good a pitcher. College scouts had their eye on him—so he probably would have gotten an athletic scholarship. I hear Danny is on the Ball State baseball team and Donnie is at Indiana Southeast. Probably the first time the twins have been apart. Jeff accepted a manager job at Auto Zone in New Albany after the boys left. The Jones family will get by. He still runs a snow plow business when needed." A dramatic sigh carried over the phone.

Blue shot Tenny a meaningful look. An unasked question, but she guessed the nature of the inquiry had to do with Hazel and gave her a nod of assent. Her friend cleared her throat before saying, "Aunt Hazel? We thought we'd swing by for a visit."

"That would be nice. With the way things are going, that will be the only positive thing in my life."

"See you soon," Blue promised and ended the call. She waited a beat and said, "She sounds awful."

"I agree. Still, isn't that what you'd expect with her daughter missing?" Tenny wondered why Hazel hadn't been more upset when they'd first met. She'd like to think if she went missing, her aunt Cinnamon would have parked herself outside the local law enforcement office and let them have no peace until she was home.

Blue mumbled something as she switched on the radio.

"What?"

"She knows where Jess is." She gave a derisive snort. "Not sure why she won't tell me. I'm *family*, after all."

"Maybe it's better. You don't want to be obstructing justice, do you?"

The truck jerked, snapping the seatbelts tight as Blue stomped on the brakes. "You're not still going with Jess' being guilty, are you?"

The thought never completely left her mind. Still, Dallas' skepticism about anyone trotting around with bags of money had merit, too. "I don't know. It just seems weird since you said it was so out of character. Then again, crimes are committed all the time by people who have never done a wrong thing in their life. Take the secretary in *Psycho*. She never stole anything and suddenly she had that huge cashier's check she had to hold onto over the weekend."

"Duh." Blue reached over the console and poked her. "Fictional character."

"I know." Tenny shrugged. "Sue me. I don't know any actual good folks who turned to a life of crime, nor do I know any hardened criminals. I have to go with fiction for examples."

A loud, prolonged beep sounded as an oversized truck whipped around them, almost taking off the Moo Town truck's extended side mirrors.

"Mercy!" Blue added something else about fools in oversized trucks, somehow missing the irony of her driving a similar vehicle. She eased her foot off the brake and drove with a tad more speed than before. "Let's go see Aunt Hazel. I need a break from all this skullduggery, especially since it isn't going anywhere. I'd like the culprit to be someone I don't share bloodlines with."

"Me, too," Tenny seconded, knowing if it did turn out to be Jess, that would put a strain on her and Blue's friendship. "Dallas implied it's all about moving numbers around. Maybe an inside job, since technically the money isn't sitting in the bank. It's not like guys in ski masks showed up with sawed-off shotguns and robbed the bank."

"I hear you," Blue commented and flipped on her signal before turning left. "You seldom hear about bank robberies. The last robbery I heard about happened at one of those mega groceries. That's where the money's at."

"Makes sense. I read about two bank employees in Clarksville who slowly siphoned off a dime here and a quarter there on the bank accounts. People who bothered to balance their checkbooks didn't get excited about such a small amount being off. They did this for almost a decade, and then the two just vanished. No goodbyes to their families. Nothing. Bank did an internal audit and discovered both women had over one hundred thousand dollars in secret accounts their families knew nothing about."

Blue snorted. "Why didn't anyone notice? Had they never done an audit before?"

"Turns out the two women who vamoosed *did* the audits. The bank manager thought it was safer to have two employees check each other's work. They probably go with outside auditors now. Anyhow, my point is, it could be an inside job. Moving numbers from one account to another. Of course, they'd eventually have to get the money out of the bank."

"I like that idea much better than Jess' being guilty."

The truck's speed slowed and stopped as a nanny goat trailing a fraying rope behind stood in the middle of the road, blocking the free flow of traffic. Blue grinned at Tenny. "Loose livestock. You know the drill."

"Yeah." Tenny twisted in her seat, searching for the nearest home. A small green tin-roofed home sat between two towering black walnut trees. "You don't think they'll shoot me?"

"Nah. Not as long as the truck isn't too close. Tell you what. I'll drive up a little farther, so I won't be seen."

"Gee, thanks." She loosened her seatbelt and slipped out the door.

Unlike Blue, farm animals frightened her a wee bit. Give her a hamster, or better yet a goldfish, and everything worked out okay. In the country, your livestock provided a living and sometimes your next meal. Courtesy demanded you return any escaping animal. A few could be troublesome. As if reading her thoughts, the goat cocked her head and bleated. She swore it said, "Forget it," but that must have been her imagination. As she drew closer, the goat watched her with those disturbing sideways pupils. she tried to snag the halter. The goat took two small steps back, foiling her attempt. The rumble of a tractor in the distance birthed hope that a farmer might be searching for a wayward goat. Only, the sound moved away as opposed to coming closer. Tenny blew out a breath. If she intended to live in the country, she'd have to rescue a few adventurous animals. She placed her hands on her hips and regarded the beast. "I bet you'd like to get back home and have a snack."

Goats maintained a reputation for eating almost anything and stomaching it, too. They were ideal critters for hardscrabble places without a lot of vegetation. Tenny patted down her pockets, certain she had tucked in a few of the cookies she bribed Precious with. Finding a few good-sized chunks, she pulled them out and flourished them in front of the goat. "Aha!"

The animal's nostrils trembled as it took in the smell and moved a few steps closer. "Yeah, I got what you want," she cooed, pushing back a hank of hair descending from her sloppy bun, making it even sloppier. Bending at the waist, she offered the cookie bits in an open left hand as her right hand reached for the halter. Her wayward hair chose that moment to flop free, gaining the goat's attention and teeth.

Her right hand curled around the halter even as she yelped in pain. "Stupid goat! What's wrong with you?"

A sharp whistle cut through the air, resulting in the goat's jerking its head back and pulling Tenny's head closer. "Stop it! I need to free my hair."

"Jezebel!" A woman's voice sounded nearby. "There you are."

From Tenny's awkward upside-down head position, she noticed a pair of worn jeans tucked into a pair of rubber farm boots with chickens and hens printed all over them. "Could you help me?"

"Glad to," the chicken-boot woman offered. "Jezebel must want to be a hairdresser." She chuckled at her own comment. "I couldn't even milk her without getting my locks thoroughly chewed."

"What did you do?" Tenny asked while bits of hair were uncomfortably extracted from Jezebel's teeth.

"Cut it all off," the woman declared, freeing the last of Tenny's tendrils.

Slowly, she lifted her head up but kept a firm grip on the halter as she faced her rescuer. "I appreciate your help."

"No problem," the woman said and ran a hand over her salt and pepper buzz cut. "My hairstyle is no work at all. The husband isn't too thrilled about it. He calls me G.I. Jane."

"I'm sure he means it in an affectionate manner," Tenny offered with a smile, anxious to get back to the truck and examine her hair, or what was left of it, more closely.

"He doesn't." She reached for the other side of the goat's halter. "No big deal to me. I call him DB 5.0. It means Dad Bod times 5. Everybody seems to be into the Dad Bod with the little tummy. My man has a huge belly, which explains the name. Anyhow, I got my goat. You can let go."

"Ah, right." Tenny released her death grip on the halter. She shot the goat a last look, knowing in the war of wills, Jezebel won. "See ya!"

"Where's your truck?" Jezebel's handler asked.

Pointing ahead, Tenny replied, "It's down the road." She broke into a jog but still heard the woman's parting remark, possibly to the goat.

"City people have no sense."

Chapter Twenty-Six

DAPPLED SUNLIGHT FILTERED by the rust, crimson, and golden autumn leaves highlighted the potholes especially those the bookmobile hit in the rainstorm of the other day. Instead of going over the dubious, aging bridge they'd used before, Blue hung a right at a narrow dirt path. Undergrowth and blackberry bushes gone wild slapped the sides of the truck. Nearby, the throaty, low rumble of a turkey vulture sounded. As a kid, she thought it sounded the way a hippotamus would. They bumped hard over the unpaved trail with mud pulling at the tires, slowing both speed and traction. When the fillings in Tenny's teeth stopped rattling and her backbone settled back into place, she let go of her held breath with a whoosh. A little calmer, but no less confused, she asked, "I understand avoiding the bridge, but do you know where we're going?"

"Got a bit of an idea."

Tenny's head pivoted ninety degrees and regarded her friend with an incredulous stare, her mouth ajar. "A bit?"

"Well, I know how you dislike the bridge."

"Wait." Tenny pointed to herself. "Don't put this on me. You're the one who said the bridge was so far gone that people wondered why it was still standing."

Blue's nose crinkled. "I may have said something like that, but not until you were over the bridge."

"Wrong!" She gave her head a hard shake. "You said it when I was in the middle of the bridge and had no place to go. Trust me, I remember."

"Huh. Should have known." She smirked and then the truck hit something, surprising a gasp out of Blue. "Better put it in four-wheel drive."

"You could have done that when you decided to go off-roading."

Blue grumbled under her breath, pushing the lever from 2-wheel to 4-wheel. "Hope this does the trick." She tapped the gas and the truck lumbered over the obstacle and then dropped roughly, bouncing both women.

"Hope that wasn't a body."

"You're so not funny. Remind me to hit the car wash on the way back. I hope there aren't any new scratches on the truck. We can't afford another paint job."

"It can be the slightly battered Holstein-looking truck."

"You're full of jokes today."

"Being stuck in a muddy wilderness on a non-road does that to me. You know, you could back up utilize your backup camera. Then turn around and use that road we went on when we left Hazel's house last time."

A grunt greeted her suggestion. Blue narrowed her eyes and kept going slowly, wincing when a branch scratched across the roof. "No reason to since we're almost there. I have the feeling Larry and Phyllis may have moved. This road hasn't been used in a while."

"Road? Talk about euphemism. It barely earns the label: cow path."

"Ha ha." Blue forced the laugh. "You'll be doing stand-up acts soon. Larry and Phyllis were one of Rivertown's founding families. Sure, they never paved the road, but they did put in a cement bridge that occasionally went under water."

Under water? Tenny's fingers wrapped around the door handle as she tried to remember the true crime episode about the kidnapped woman in the back seat of a car that sank into a lake. Was the window open so she had a better chance of swimming out? As a precaution, she pressed the window lever, lowering the window.

"What are you doing? Put up that window before you get slapped by a branch or a varmint jumps in. There could be snakes in the branches."

Tenny regarded the trees with a suspicious eye. No snakes or wildlife were in sight, but a few trees gave off an air they weren't to be messed with—which could be the result of too many fantasy books. Death by drowning or being slapped in the face by a tree. She'd almost decided on the tree when Blue whooped.

"There it is!"

A narrow stream of turbulent water whipped by the front of the truck. Almost level with the water was a basic cement bridge. There were no guard rails, and puddles of water dotted the narrow width. "We're in luck. It's still intact."

Why didn't Tenny feel lucky? She cut her eyes to Blue, who grinned and proceeded slowly over the bridge. Almost unaware of her actions, Tenny raised her feet like she did when she was young to keep her feet from getting wet. A child's game really, but she kept her feet up and her window down. The front wheels of the truck found purchase on the other side about the time a cracking noise came from behind and Blue floored it. The truck rumbled up the path with a mechanical groan. Once all four wheels were firmly on the ground, the two of them glanced back at the bridge.

A huge V-shaped gap resulted in water bubbling over the bridge and chewing away at the rest of it. Blue reached over and grabbed Tenny's hand and squeezed. "I should have listened to you instead of cowgirling it."

This could be a big *I told you so* moment, but they weren't out of the woods yet, figuratively and literally. "We should be close to Hazel's house."

"That's what I hope."

Pines lined the path, some tall and scraggly while others remained short and half dead. The path widened, making the rest of the drive less nerve-wracking except for a few grinding moments in the mud, but they both remained inside. It would have worked out better if she'd closed the window before they hit the mud. Around ten minutes later, they pulled up to Hazel's ranch house.

Aunt Hazel, attired in a red jogging suit with the emblem of a local collegiate team, exited her front door, strolled to the truck, and greeted them. She patted her red hair, graying at the roots, that she had pulled into an untidy chignon. When Tenny climbed out of the truck, Hazel laughed. The mud-dotted clothes, the red welt on her face from the wayward branch she'd been warned about, plus her goat-chewed hair, failed to make the best impression.

"Oh my!" Hazel giggled again. "I thought I looked bad, but you look *so* much worse."

It was hard to know what to say to that. There was no polite response, so on to the next subject, Tenny asked, "Did something happen?"

Blue exited the truck, squatted, and checked the undercarriage as her aunt explained. "Buck Adler. That no-account con artist backed out of buying my house, that's what! It's what I get for being honest."

"I assume you told him the government already paid for it."

She perched one hand on her hip and gave a toss of her head. "What they say and what they do is two different things. There was talk of compensating us for our land. Money I'll never see."

"Banks are insured by the Federal Deposit Insurance Corporation for up to two hundred and fifty thousand dollars per account," Tenny said and added with a brow lift, "Had a student working in finance. At least, I hope he was majoring in finance."

Her brow furrowed as she considered all the information she'd given in good faith, that they were pursuing a research project and not a life of crime. She shrugged off the thought and returned to the original conversation. "I'd assume each person got a specific price for their home. More property means more money. You should still have the money, but it may take more time to get it through the FDIC. Did they say where the money would be deposited?"

Hazel's eyes rolled up. "The town council used Granite Savings and Loan. Not sure if the government check would go to the same place." Her tongue darted out to lick her lips. "I like the sounds of that. FDIC insurance. Means I have money out there somewhere. So much better than the bogus offer from the would-be crystal trader."

Blue, done examining the truck for scratches and dents, moved to her aunt and hugged her. "What's this about a crystal trader?"

"Buck. Turns out he thought it was rich in minerals. The crystal people are paying big money for certain crystals. You know, like in Sedona. Heard a decent quartz point could go for thirty dollars." She held her thumb and forefinger about an inch apart. "Nothing big. California folks show and buy everything crystal they can get their hands on.'" She put her hands on the small of her back. "Buck thought this property would make him into a crystal king."

Blue wiggled her fingers, working out the kinks from white-knuckling the steering wheel. "Where'd he get an idea like that?"

"Jess."

"How so?" Tenny inquired, speculating that everything circled back to Jess.

"She collected all these crystals when she was little. Used to beg me to take her to rock shows. Then one day about a month ago, she tells me she was going to return them to the earth. That's a thing now." Hazel sniffed before continuing, "She takes her boxes outside and scatters all those expensive crystals through the woods surrounding our house. I suppose my would-be buyer found the crystals and thought there had to be many more underneath. His offer came because he thought the place was full of clear crystal quartz points and clusters. When he asked me about it, I told him Indiana wasn't known for clear quartz, just calcite." Her shoulders went up into a shrug. "He stomped off."

Blue clicked her tongue. "I doubt he had the money to buy the property to begin with."

"Probably not," Aunt Hazel agreed. "I want to know more about getting money for my land."

Tenny held up one hand. "I'm not sure about this. It depends if the money was put in individual accounts or what. It would be a lot easier if we could talk to Jess. Surely, she has a clue."

"Yeah, about that," Hazel said. "She should be back in the country in a couple of days."

Chapter Twenty-Seven

BLUE, TENNY, AND Hazel stood near the mud-spattered Moo Town truck. Both younger women's eyes widened and their mouths gaped as Hazel gestured with her hands as if waving away her previous comment about her daughter's being out of the country. A pair of crows landed in a nearby tree with a flutter and a scrabble as they chose a roosting spot.

"Country?" Blue whispered the word at the same time as a crow called. Reading her lips, Tenny echoed the sentiment and elaborated on it. "You mean Jess left the country?"

"Oh." Hazel threw up her hands. "I've said too much. It's supposed to be a secret. No one is supposed to know."

Aunt Hazel headed for the house. Tenny glanced at her friend and raised an eyebrow, which resulted in Blue's hurrying after her aunt. "Wait! You can't say something like that and just leave. It doesn't work like that."

A screen door banged after Hazel's hasty entrance and slammed again after Blue. Family matters, Tenny rationalized, as she stood outside and leaned back against the truck, forgetting for a second about the mud. Remembering, she pushed off the vehicle, brushing off new mud clumps. An avian feud broke out above her with the crows growing more vocal and flapping their wings. Then again, they might be giving her advice. She watched them as they settled and glared at her. One gave a strident *caw*, which could have been the equivalent of *go*, or that's how she translated it.

Once inside, boxes surrounded the sofa where Hazel and Blue perched. Using a tissue to dab at her eyes, Hazel sniffed. "I promised not to tell."

"I understand." Blue reached for her aunt's hand. "I think Jess wouldn't mind my knowing."

"You're not going to say anything, are you?"

Blue visibly inhaled and then smiled. "I'll keep your secret."

"What?" Tenny felt as if she had come in on the second act of a play. In a way, she had. Apparently, she misunderstood the crow and it actually meant *stay* as opposed to *go*. Hazel and Blue, both a little glassy-eyed, turned toward Tenny.

"Secret?" She repeated the troublesome word that might possibly lead to her bestie's being on the wrong side of the law. Family is family, but sometimes friends needed to serve as first responders in thorny dilemmas like this. Tenny crossed her arms and straightened to her full five foot eight inches as if that might intimidate. That would only work if someone didn't know her, but even then, it was somewhat doubtful. "So, what's this secret you're keeping?"

Blue shot her aunt a questioning look. Hazel shrugged her shoulders and said, "Might as well tell her. Everyone in the county knows you can't keep a secret, which is why Jess didn't tell you. She started to and sent you a text. Remember?"

A mulish expression settled around Blue's mouth, pulling her lips down. "It was hard to forget. The text had the air of kidnapping."

"No, it didn't." Hazel disagreed and lifted her chin. "She would have texted *I'm being kidnapped.* I didn't raise a fool. Just a tender-hearted gal who wants to protect her friend."

"The bank robber," Tenny inserted as she tried to put the pieces of the puzzle together. So far, she considered the movement of money to be an inside job, which put Jess out of the loop, but what if she knew the thief, who probably told her a sob story?

"No!" Blue answered, stood, and stretched, prolonging her explanation. "Aunt Hazel just told me the truth. Jess' best friend, Kelly, was supposed to get married last week. Not an elaborate ceremony, thank goodness. A little church wedding with the reception in the basement. Cake and punch and all that."

"Okay." Tenny flaked off a piece of drying mud from her face that had started to itch during the curious explanation. "Not sure how this has anything to do with vanishing funds."

Blue huffed and fisted both hands on her hips. "Not *everything* has to do with the relocation money. Try to follow."

Weren't their semi-disastrous trips to Rivertown about finding the funds, the thief, and the missing cousin? Blue now acted as if all their work was merely an impulsive activity rather like a mani-pedi or a movie matinee. Her attitude irked. The problem with being a natural redhead was irritation flushed her face, making her upset obvious. She pulled her shirt away from her chest, shaking it a little. "It's hot in here."

Blue chuckled. "I know you're mad, but when you hear the whole story, it will make sense."

"If you say so." Spying a chair, Tenny removed a box and sat. Gesturing to Blue, she said, "Enlighten me."

Blue's chin lifts the tiniest bit and she spreads her open hands wide as if opening a book or beginning an epic tale. "First, you should know Kelly and Jess have been friends forever. They started kindergarten together, joined Girl Scouts, and—"

"Is there a condensed version?"

"It's better with the intro," Blue explained, then snorted. "I'll cut to the chase for you. Anyhow, Kelly fell hard for a local bad boy who I won't bother to name because I don't even want to say his name."

Tenny circled her hand for her to wind it up. She wanted evidence that her friend hadn't stepped over to the felonious side. "Don't say his name."

"Hmph," Blue muttered. "I will call him hereafter as Jerk Face. Jerk Face broke up with Kelly two weeks before the wedding. Took off with some chick he met at the casino. He's out of town, and Kelly is left to tidy up things. She told her mama, of course, who told her mother to stop cooking. The minister got a phone call that there wouldn't be any wedding."

So far, nothing fit in with Jess' being gone. "Out of the country?"

"Not sure if Kelly had doubts about Jerk Face, but she kept the honeymoon reservations in her name only. Kelly and Jess headed out to Mexico a couple of days early to avoid seeing the confused people who showed up at church expecting a wedding. Now, some of them could have heard from Jerk Face's family about his calling it off, but I doubt it because that would involve some responsibility on his part, which isn't his strong suit. Anyhow, Kelly and Jess are on their way back."

It didn't take a math genius to count back the days to when the wedding should have been and Jess' flight. "Shouldn't the failed marriage ceremony have happened already, and Kelly's mama informed everyone there wasn't going to be a wedding?"

Hazel cocked her head as if considering the matter. "You're

right. I didn't go, since I already knew there wouldn't be a wedding. Besides, I might see a few of those old biddies who badmouthed my girl."

"Well," Tenny started again. "I assume everyone in Rivertown knows. It isn't a secret anymore."

Chuckles erupted along with a few grins. Relief flooded Tenny. She so hated her hasty assumption that she might have to serve as a character witness for her bestie. Hazel placed a hand over her heart. "Good thing, too, since everyone knows Blue can't keep a secret to save her life."

Chapter Twenty-Eight

THE SUN, AFTER reaching its zenith and sending out drying heat rays to the damp landscape, dipped toward the western horizon. Both Blue and Tenny left a smiling Hazel and headed for the Moo Town truck. The day felt lighter after understanding the reason behind Jess' sudden flight. Maybe in her rush, Jess simply forgot her phone. Tenny pursed her lips as she considered the possibility. "Do you think Jess texted from Kelly's number?"

"That makes sense," Blue commented as she opened the driver's side door. Both women climbed inside, shut their doors, and turned to wave goodbye.

Parts of the puzzle fit, but some other pieces were just plain missing. "Are you satisfied about Jess?" Tenny asked.

"Typical. I should have expected as much. She's young and impulsive but good at heart." Blue chuckled and stuck out her tongue. "Can you believe there was a moment I had my doubts?"

There was no need to mention her thoughts on the subject. Of course, if Jess were guilty of heading to Mexico and hiding money in a foreign bank, that could work, too. After all, banks were guilty of money laundering—although most didn't know. No one showed up with a deposit slip and money mentioning a felony in the process. At least, she suspected they wouldn't. With a quick peek at her friend, sitting straight and beaming after receiving the "secret" news, Tenny decided not to share her reservations.

Instead, she watched the trees slip by as they headed in the direction of the river. "I wonder how Fred is doing? I'm supposed to pick him up today."

"Better call the vet now. We'll be out of cell phone range soon."

Good advice. Remembering her recent trip down this road, she put the vet's number into her phone. The phone rang twice and the vet's receptionist and wife picked up. "Hello?"

"It's Tenny. I dropped Fred the frog off and was coming back to pick him up today. Just wondering how he was doing?"

A long pause worried Tenny. People seldom hesitated when they had good news. Even though Fred originated as Blue's project, she still felt a responsibility for him—mainly assuring he wasn't eaten by Precious—but a responsibility all the same.

"The vet is out at a farm delivering twin foals. No reason for you to make the trip, though."

Tenny gulped, catching the attention of Blue, who mouthed, "what?" She settled for saying, "Fred," a little bit above a whisper.

"Oh, he's fine. Better than fine, I'd say. The vet gave him a steroid shot that had him hopping with no problem. He decided to check out his swimming abilities in the pond behind the clinic where an army of frogs live. He swam away with the other frogs. No getting him back either. I'd say he's happy where he is. You're more than welcome to try to pick him out from the other frogs if you can."

They'd lost her frog—make that Blue's frog. "Umm, no. What do I owe you?"

"Don't worry about it. We tend not to charge people when we lose the patient."

"Does this happen often?"

"You're the first and hopefully the last. He probably has his eye on a lady frog. Consider his happiness."

She pushed a tendril of hair out of her face. "You're right. His happiness is paramount. Goodbye."

Her thumb disconnected the call before she even heard the final farewell. She sniffed, patted her pockets for a tissue, and finding a slightly used one, wiped one eye. How could she be attached to the frog that she only had for a day at most?

Blue cleared her throat. "I'm sorry about Fred."

"He's okay," Tenny assured. "Fine enough to swim off with some other frogs."

"That's good, right?"

"It is. Much better than my making certain he didn't become a raccoon snack."

Blue made a *tsking* noise. "That would require Precious' actually hunting for his own food, which I doubt he'll do as long as you keep providing home-cooked meals for him."

"Don't rag on me—you picked up the worst dog in the world and decided he needed you."

"Come on." Blue pushed her thumb into Tenny's side. "He's not the worst. By the time we get to Canine Stampede, he'll be a well-behaved companion."

"I like Marvin, but I doubt he's going to transform your pup into Lassie in a few hours. Feels like all talk to me."

"I suspect as much." She pushed off her cap and ran one hand through her hair, fluffing it. "If he were in the transforming business, we could use a herder like a blue heeler."

Even though the temptation to ask *why not get the type of dog they needed* came close to slipping out of her mouth, she didn't follow through. One of the reasons Blue and Tenny became friends was Blue probably saw her as the motherless girl who needed a friend, which was true. It was best to speak of things not related to the mischievous Sir Moolah. "You still want to find the thief?"

"Nah, I'm good. Let the professionals handle it."

Unsure if she'd misheard or perhaps her friend chose to prank her, Tenny twisted in her seat to face Blue. "Did I hear you right? You don't care if the thief escapes punishment?"

"That's not what I said." Blue sucked in her lips for a few seconds and then blew out an audible breath. "Jess is not guilty, and that's all I care about."

After investing three anxiety-filled days on the search, Tenny couldn't just give it up. "You know people will still consider Jess guilty unless the crime is pinned on someone."

Blue drove silently and then slapped the wheel. "I hate it when you're right. Any big ideas about who it is? I know today's look-see yielded nothing."

That's the problem with pointing out the lack of a culprit—people expected you to snap your fingers and produce one. "You remember the story I told you about the bank employees literally nickel and diming bank customers for years?"

"Yeah," Blue acknowledged, "but that took over a decade."

"They were careful." Tenny sniffed. "Our thief or thieves may be in a hurry, which should make them easier to catch. Your aunt mentioned the bank." She blew out a breath, ruffling her bangs. "It was something about a rock. With regional banks, their websites feature employees' faces and job titles. It makes their bank appear friendly."

"Not sure I ever looked up a bank website before. Seems like it won't be that much help."

"Maybe not. Still, it's a place to start, especially if it's a smaller local bank. Do you remember the name?"

They hit a pothole, which resulted in Blue's mumbling about the suspension system. "I was checking out the truck at the time you were showing off your financial knowledge."

"Well, all I remember is it was named after a rock. That's not all that helpful."

"Sure, it is. How many banks can there be named after rocks?" Blue shrugged. "It's not as if we are in the big city. How many banks can there be?"

"A few." Tenny played with bank names. Rock Solid? No, that sounded like one of those muscle-building supplements advertised on late-night television. The Rock? Nope. That sounded more like a few churches she'd driven past. Often, they had an oversized rock on their sign, and one actually had a boulder with a cross attached to it. "Limestone! You know this area is associated with limestone."

"Limestone Bank?" Blue said and then shook her head. "It doesn't feel familiar. Keep thinking. We're almost to Canine Stampede and closer to my pooch. You'll be so overwhelmed with his skills that you'll forget all about the bank."

"I doubt it."

They drove the last few miles with Blue chattering about the wonders of a well-trained Moolah. According to her fantasy, he'd be ready for dog food commercials or a career in the movies. Everyone knew they didn't have enough cute, trained dogs in Hollywood.

This time when they entered Canine Stampede's parking lot, there were a couple more cars than before, possibly dog owners that were here to pick up their pets. One happened to be a rose petal pink Volkswagen beetle, complete with artificial eyelashes on the headlights. On the side of the car was a magnetic sign with a beribboned cartoon poodle and the words: *Isabelle's Dog Mobile Grooming*, along with a phone number.

An older man with a cane was easing out of the passenger side of an oversized SUV. Standing close by, a dark-haired younger woman tried to help but was shooed off—probably a relative. They made their way to the front door.

Blue noticed them and pointed to them. "Wonder what kind of dog they have? I'm going to say a pug or a Boston Terrier. How about you?"

A smaller white pickup truck with a toolbox mounted on the bed caught her eye, if only for the name stenciled on it: *Granite Savings and Loan*.

Instead of answering with an iconic breed or mutt, Tenny pointed to the truck. "Look!"

"It's a truck. On the small side, too." She shot Tenny a quizzical glance as she parked near the vehicle. "Do you need a truck?"

"The name. Granite Savings and Loan!"

"That's it!"

Chapter Twenty-Nine

T HE TREES, STILL holding onto their colorful leaves, shaded part of the Canine Stampede exercise area and building. Dogs inside the fenced play yard barked with excitement when Blue and Tenny exited the truck. Blue strolled to the fence, watching the dogs play. Inside the yard were stairs and hurdles for dog training. Several filled water dishes waited underneath a tree. Three benches sat scattered about, possibly for visitors.

One petite white dog sat on a bench with the posture of a princess while a huskie mix and a Golden chased each other. The little white dog acted bored with the other dogs' antics. Tenny knew what her friend hoped to find. "No Moolah. He must be inside getting trained."

"You're right." Blue touched the fence and stared at the dogs. "With Fred the frog swimming away, I was almost afraid we'd arrive and there would be no Moolah."

"That's just silly. No one is going to steal that dog." She pressed her lips together, thinking she should lighten the mood, and added, "You're good unless he's going to *swim* away."

"Yeah, not happening." She sighed and smoothed her hands over her shirt.

"What's wrong?" The earlier euphoria at finding out Jess' disappearance wasn't abduction or evading the law had faded fairly fast.

"Oh, you know." She turned away from the dogs and gazed out at the road. "I can be a bit impulsive."

"Just a bit," Tenny teased, trying to pull a smile from her friend.

"A lot, then." She walked a few steps and then turned and walked back to Tenny. Using three fingers, she tapped her chest. "I guess that's why I can understand Jess' behavior. My heart is in the right place."

"No one questioned that."

She inhaled audibly, then let it out. "Yeah, but it doesn't serve me. I'm hoping I'll walk into that lobby and Moolah will be a totally different dog. One that doesn't sour the milk or drive Griffin crazy. Deep down, I know it isn't so. No matter how I might want something, it doesn't always make it happen."

Tenny wanted to agree a hundred percent with Moolah's not changing in a couple of hours. Despite the impracticality of Moolah's becoming an obedience star, Tenny needed something that would cheer her friend. "What about Jess? You wanted her to be safe and not a robber." She flourished her hands as if performing a magic act. "Et voilà! She is."

"I'll give you that." Blue popped up an index finger. "Jess wasn't a wild sort to begin with, which is the reason I couldn't understand why people blamed her. Makes you understand why no one ever wants to hold positions within an organization. Moolah, on the other hand…" She left the sentence uncompleted.

Even though she didn't complete the sentence, Tenny, knowing her friend as she did, could fill in the missing words. As impulsive and kind-hearted as Blue could be, she had a practical side, too. That side knew she couldn't hold onto a dog that soured the dairy business and strained her relationship with her husband. The dog training plan only put off the inevitable decision.

"Let's go inside and see how he is. We may both be surprised. One day at a time. That's all you can do."

Blue smirked and pointed her finger at Tenny. "Same to you as far as your bookmobile service and a certain sunflower farmer."

"Yeah, that." She grimaced, not willing to delve into either topic.

Pivoting together as if they were a two-person marching band, they turned toward the front of the building as a man, possibly in his late thirties, exited—not bad looking if the furrowed brow and frowning lips could morph into something a little less intense. Dressed in dark jeans and a windbreaker, he struck a memory. Where had she seen him before? She watched him climb into the white truck and leave.

"You know that guy?"

Blue answered with a shrug as they made their way to the lobby. With her hand on the door, she said, "Wait! I think that's the guy from the gas station from a couple of days ago. I told you he was cute, just to get your reaction. You were so not interested."

"I remember now. He was driving a different vehicle."

"Sportscar. That, I remember, since no one in Rivertown would have such an impractical vehicle with the roads being what they are."

Weird. She considered the man, the car, and the fact that he was driving a Granite Savings and Loan truck. Was it all a coincidence his being wherever they were? Maybe she was falling into a conspiracy mindset, seeing connections where there were none.

As Blue opened the door, happy voices babbled along with the chirp of a *bow-wow* door alarm. The older man they'd spied in the parking lot sat in Marvin's rocking chair with Moolah on his lap. The dog snuggled against the man, acting as if he were a transformed dog. Marvin must be a miracle worker. The younger woman stood behind the chair with her hand on the man's shoulder.

"We can't thank you enough. Rascal means the world to my father, especially after my mother's death. I've cautioned Dad about taking him everywhere. It only opens up more opportunities for the adventurous dog to escape. I certainly never thought anyone would take him."

Blue stiffened up beside Tenny, and her eyes narrowed. Well aware of what the outcome could be, she latched onto her friend's arm and whispered, "Find out the story before going in guns blazing."

"I'm okay," Blue insisted and tried to shake off her grasp.

"Not believing it. I'll just hold on. Griffin will thank me."

Marvin spotted them and waved them closer. "Ah look! It's the sweet woman who has been taking care of Rascal."

The woman responded first with a knife-sharp glare and equally biting words. "Why didn't you have him wanded?"

Feeling Blue's muscles bunch under her arms, Tenny chose to answer. "Blue only had Rascal a couple of days. An urgent family matter has taken precedence over searching for an owner, but I do know Griffin made inquiries using Pet Finder."

"Griffin?" The woman repeated the name. "Oh, yes, he's the gentleman who called and told me where to find my father's dog."

The older man cradling Moolah murmured, "Bless you," as a tear rolled down his wrinkled cheek. "It's been difficult this last week, not knowing what happened to my Rascal." He backhanded a tear as the dog rested on his lap on the edge of falling asleep. "He's an energetic pup, and I know I don't provide enough exercise for him." He shook his head slowly. "He decided to make his own adventure. Unfortunately, he's not good at finding his way home. Wish we had a place like Canine Stampede in Beechnut. It would allow Rascal some fun without taking a few years off my limited span."

Blue kept silent, but Tenny knew she had questions, such as, *how do we know it's your dog?* Tenny smiled at the couple. "I can tell you love Rascal a lot. When did you get him?"

The daughter spoke before her father could—Tenny suspected she probably did that a great deal. "One of my co-workers' dogs had puppies. She found homes for all the puppies except one. We'd lost my mother a few months earlier to cancer, and everyone struggled with the loss. I thought a puppy might help. A soft, cuddly, adorable puppy."

The man fondled the sleeping dog's ears and smirked. "That's what she thought it would be. Rascal earned his name, chewing up everything in sight. Sometimes, I think I should have named him Goat. Some folks might call him a slow learner, but I'm okay with that. None too fast myself. It's comforting to have his warm body next to me in the easy chair when we watch television. *Golden Girls* is one of his favorites. He wakes me up in the morning with a lick on the face, which helps because at night I take off my glasses and hearing aid, which makes me practically blind and deaf."

The bunched muscles in Blue's arms eased and a sideways glance revealed her friend absorbing the story with a trembling lip. Anymore heart-warming anecdotes and she'd be bawling. Tenny decided to end the tales with a comment. "Sounds like you really missed him. Glad you found each other."

Blue, being calm, pried Tenny's fingers off her arm and offered, "I have a carrier in the truck."

The man held up his hand. "We brought Rascal's carrier. You keep yours because I suspect someone with a heart as caring as yours will find a new animal to love."

At that exact moment, the door opened, bringing with it the sound of high-pitched barking and the smell of autumn. A small, fluffy dog charged, resulting in its elderly owner dropping its sequined encrusted lead in surprise.

Tenny volunteered, "I'll get him," before she dashed off after the little escapee. Several voices responded, including Marvin, who insisted he could catch the animal. After working with Moolah, Tenny felt competent to corner the wayward dog and return it to its owner.

The fast canine disappeared, forcing Tenny's pace to slow as she peered into each room. One door half opened exposed a damp wash area complete with a grooming table and the smell of wet dog. There was no canine in sight, but Tenny picked up the towels just to be sure.

The clatter of canine nails on concrete caught her attention and propelled her down the long hallway, checking empty kennels without luck. The last door in the hallway stood ajar a few inches, just enough room for a pint-sized pooch to slip through. She placed her hand on the door and pushed. Inside was a desk with an open laptop resting on top. A desk chair had been pushed back as if the recent occupant left in a hurry. That sounded like someone who'd recently rushed out of Canine Stampede.

Curious. Pulling a tissue from her pocket, she wrapped it around her index finger and touched the mouse. The screen fluttered to life, showing a bank account balance of Louis B. Butterworth. Her mouth gaped as she noticed the money amount. Mr. Butterworth's net worth could buy and sell Rivertown. The only question was, *who was Mr. Butterworth?*

A whimper drew her gaze to the small dog huddled near several taped-up boxes. She scooped up the dog, noticing hidden behind it, a portable firesafe with a handle. Even more curious. She padded out of the room, anxious to get far away and contemplate what she'd found at a much safer distance. Her heart pounded as she peered both ways and then pulled the door closed using a shirt-wrapped hand. Maybe she might mess up the fingerprints, but at least hers wouldn't be on them.

As she moved closer to the lobby, Marvin showed up and demanded, "Where were you?"

Definitely less friendly than he had been before. Tenny swallowed and held up the small dog. "Finding your newest customer. Got stuck in one of the kennel rooms."

"Good job." He managed a smile, but his eyes failed to pick up the message and still telegraphed his ire.

Inside the lobby, the newest visitor lit up when Tenny presented her with her pet.

"My little Caesar is a wild one. Always trying to claim new territory." She chuckled.

Blue stood near the door, looking out of place and weary. All the same, she wished Rascal's original owner well and left, but Tenny waited a second, not wanting to dash off as if she had a juicy tidbit. Instead, she feigned everything was normal. "You certainly changed that dog around."

"No." His nose crinkled along with his crow's feet. "I'd like to take credit, but I imagine the doggy was just plain homesick as opposed to being ornery."

"Oh, by the way. What do we owe you?" She kept chattering, hoping to ease into the subject she wanted, even if she ended up paying for the dog's training.

"The happy dog owners paid me. Seeing the man and dog greet each other was actually payment enough. His daughter insisted, calling it a finder's fee."

If she hadn't seen for herself how content Moolah/Rascal was, she'd have wondered if this wasn't a scam. People found dogs, kept them, and waited for the real owners to offer a reward before coming forward. Suddenly, she suspected everyone of nefarious doings, but very few earned the dubious honor. "I noticed when we came a nice-looking guy climbing into a Granite Bank truck."

"Oh, him." Marvin pushed back his shoulders and winked. "That's my Lloyd. As much as I appreciate your plain speaking, he's tangled up with that high-maintenance gal who could benefit from a manner class and driving lessons. If you're willing to wait, she'll probably chuck him to the side once she's done with him."

Tenny forced a laugh as wheels started to churn in her head. "I'll keep that in mind." She pushed open the door, waved, and then jogged to the running truck, now parked in front of the walkway. When she opened the truck door, she boosted herself in and announced, "I have a suspect *and* motivation."

Chapter Thirty

T HE SUN-WARMED INTERIOR of the truck felt welcome as Tenny slid into the Moo Town truck, pulling the door closed behind her. Raised eyebrows, pursed lips revealed Blue's open curiosity as she waited for Tenny's elaboration on the thief's identity comment. "Start driving. I'll tell you as we go."

Blue groaned dramatically and shoved the truck into drive. "Make me wait."

"Yeah, yeah." Tenny twisted in her seat, trying to spot anyone watching them drive away. No one, which worked. After they drove a couple of miles and paused at a four-way stop, Blue made a point of clearing her throat. "Are you going to tell me now?"

"I can." Something moving in her side view mirror distracted her. A dusty, silver Mercedes came up fast, almost on their bumper, but stopped in time. "Hey! You think that's Rita behind us?"

Before Blue could answer, the car whipped around them with a long horn blare.

"Sounds like her," Blue remarked.

"Makes me wonder what she's up to so far from home. Marvin told me his son was involved with Rita, and he's none too pleased about it. I think he called me an honest speaker or something like that. As compliments go, it's a bit on the underwhelming side." She blew out a breath. "Rita and Marvin's son."

"I pity the man." Blue snorted, turning slightly and addressing her friend. "You know she had standards. With her parents' latest financial failure, she'll be on the hunt for a man with money. Is Marvin's son well-off?"

"I don't know." She watched the Mercedes grow smaller and smaller until it was no more. "He does work at the bank that Rivertown's money vanished from."

"And?" Blue prompted with an interested expression. "Please tell me Rita's involved, and my day will be perfect."

"Love to, but I can't. So far, nothing, unless the son wanted to make himself more Rita's type with a flashy show of money and an eye-catching sports car."

Blue slapped the wheel. "Why hasn't Karma caught up with that woman? She's spread her brand of snarky charm across the county. Shouldn't some of it come back to bite her?"

"I hear you." Tenny fiddled with a spoon ring on her right hand. The ring had been a favorite of her aunt's and by wearing it, she felt closer to Cinnamon. "My aunt would tell me not to concentrate on the bad someone else did, but to worry about my own actions."

Blue narrowed her eyes. "I bet she didn't mean Rita when she said that."

They both laughed so hard that tears formed in the corner of their eyes. Finally, Blue gasped. "Stop it. I have to drive."

"All right. I was thinking that Marvin is so proud of his son. He helped him get the loan for the Canine Stampede." A snort greeted the statement, but she continued her theory. "Or did he? Maybe he just moved some money around."

A heavy wind blew across the road, sending leaves skittering and buffeting the truck. Up ahead, most of the trees stood shorn of their leaves and remained dark silhouettes with their limbs stretched skyward as if beseeching. "Could be," Blue concluded. "Marvin mentioned that he did something with computers. I did notice the son looked upset when he left today. Perhaps he's regretting his actions."

"Maybe. I think it's more likely he keeps something inside Canine Stampede. Possibly the missing money. With everyone coming and going, he couldn't get to it. That explains why Lloyd and Rita keep meeting there." The unlikelihood of style-setter Rita showing up at a kennel not once, but twice, and possibly even more, had to involve something that would benefit the blonde. Tenny groaned, "I don't want Marvin to get hurt."

"He won't if he's not involved."

A fair point. Tenny pursed her lips and considered how she might further investigate Marvin's son. There was the tip line. Usually, you didn't have to give your name, and often nothing came of the information. Hers might just be another crazy call with absolutely no value. Then again, Marvin was so proud of his son, maybe he was as clever as his father bragged. As an IT bank employee, Lloyd could cover his tracks, especially since he chose to stay in the area and play the long game. Even though Tenny never considered herself a fan of felonious behavior, she had to admit it served as the smarter action. Those who flee immediately after a crime often end up apprehended.

"Maybe," Tenny mused as she watched the passing scenery, "I'll just let the system work out who's the guilty party. There's too many loose ends with Marvin ending up with an expensive business without any real effort, his son driving an expensive sports car, and dating Rita, who has very pricey tastes. Lloyd just happens to work at the bank the money vanished from, and it has all the earmarks of an inside job. I stumbled into the office at Canine Stampede and found a laptop open to a Mr. Butterworth's account, who happens to have lots of money. Makes me wonder who Mr. Butterworth is?"

Blue gave her the side eye. "Computer just happened to be on that?"

"It may have cycled off." She grimaced. "Chair was pushed away as if a person darted away for some reason. There was even one of those fire safes you carry around just in case your house catches on fire, or you have very important documents to move, such as ones with Ben Franklin's photos on them."

"I suppose I should lecture you about snooping," Blue teased.

"Looking for a dog."

"So, you say." Blue sucked in her lips for a second and then added, "I was busy feeling sorry for myself even though I knew my Moolah was really Rascal, and he was going to where he needed to be. All the same, I could tell Marvin wasn't pleased when you charged after the dog."

"Yeah, I got that feeling, too. I assured him I found the dog in the kennel, but for a moment, his folksy attitude vanished. He tried to get it back, and I did my best to act as if everything was okay."

"Sounds a bit on the scary side. As for Mr. Butterworth's account, was there enough money in the account to cover the missing funds?"

"More." A sigh escaped Tenny. "Could be a bogus account. If not, how could Lloyd or Marvin pull up someone else's account?"

"Didn't Marvin say his son worked with the computer systems at the bank? If anyone would know how to hack into an account, a computer whiz would."

A cold chill climbed up Tenny's back. She tried to shake it off without luck. Sucking in a deep breath, she said, "I could be wrong, but let's have the professionals who get paid for this stuff have a whack at it. Now all I need is a public phone to call from."

"That might be even harder to find than a suspect," Blue joked. "I think I saw one at a gas station closer to Emerson. It might still be there. Better know your number because I can guarantee they won't have a phone book. If it's there, I'll provide distraction. There's plenty of folks with big ears hoping for a choice piece of gossip. It might be the second favorite activity in Emerson."

"What's the first?" She expected a sweet response such as attending the homecoming game or picking apples in the fall.

"Grousing about Rita and how she ruins everything." Blue chuckled. "You should see your face. I don't know why you act so surprised."

"It's not apple pie and kittens with ribbons. I expected something sweeter from you."

A combination of a cough and snort came from Blue. "I think today I'm allowed a few snarky comments. You do what you need to do, and hopefully, we can pin the crime on the culprit."

Twenty minutes later, the gas station sign came into view, along with a mini-mart with a pay phone outside stuck on the wall like an afterthought. Two vehicles waited at the fuel pumps and through the glass window, a customer, clutching an oversized drink, could be seen chatting with the cashier. There weren't too many people here and most would be leaving soon. Perfect timing for her anonymous tipster call.

Chapter Thirty-One

THE SCREECH OF a blue jay shattered Tenny's dream about sitting in a rowboat while Dallas rowed. Her finger trailed in the cool water while an oversized hat shadowed her face. It could have served as a commercial for something that took you from reality to a fantasy world. The bird calls morphed into a more upbeat chirp of a robin. Ah yes, the mockingbird. A quick peep at the glowing numerals of her bedside clock showed her feathered friend started his concert at barely five in the morning. No wonder so many people trash-talked the bird. If only they'd start their morning recitals a little later.

Darkness huddled in the corners. The lighted outline of the bedroom door drew her attention. It meant she forgot to turn off a light somewhere in the house. It wasn't too surprising after her tipster call. The operator sounded none too thrilled with her info. Maybe she didn't believe the Mr. Butterworth account at Granite Bank and the sudden possession of a luxury sportscar were connected. She probably considered her another bored person with nothing else to do but make up bogus tips. What concerned her more was if someone suspected her and Blue of reporting on Lloyd. Can't say driving around a bookmobile or a truck that resembled a dairy cow could be termed low-key. Even though Hazel accused Blue of being a blabbermouth, she suspected the aunt indulged in rumor-mongering, too. She might be quick to point fingers—not sure if any would point at Lloyd, though.

As a woman alone in a patch of the county with no law presence, she played with the idea of an alarm system. Most of the thefts involved anhydrous ammonia fertilizer by would-be meth makers. Occasionally, license plates disappeared, which may be more of a high school prank. Whenever anything of value vanished such as a car, locals always blamed city folks.

Maybe a guard dog that was neither intimidated by nor would try to eat Precious could help. Outside, something thumped on the porch, followed by another louder thump, and an explosion of glass.

"Precious!" She growled the word as she rolled out of bed. She hadn't seen the animal when she returned, but had left out some water and Captain Crunch cereal. Apparently, that wasn't good enough. As far as his sleeping inside, she was not a fan unless he had a gated carrier. Tenny slid her feet into her slippers but didn't bother with her glasses, since she wasn't going to *read* him the riot act. She chuckled at her own joke and grabbed the broom as she passed the kitchen on her way to the front of the house where the sound originated. The screen door creaked open under her hand, and she peered out onto the porch illuminated by a half-moon and a security light. With no sign of Precious on the right side, she pivoted left, but before she could search for her raccoon, a hard jerk to the head caused her to stumble. Someone grabbed her hair plait and pulled her backward, resulting in her hitting the siding.

A cool, metallic point slid under her chin, barely pricking her skin as a warm breath fanned her cheek. "Why did you come back?"

Despite the words being growled, Tenny recognized the speaker.

Unlike her usual coping mechanism of changing the subject, instinct warned her to say nothing. She blinked and inhaled slowly, trying to calm herself and figure a way out of the predicament without a knife in the throat result.

Perfume wafted from her attacker, which tickled her nose. Tenny sucked her lips in, trying not to sneeze as the woman continued her tirade. "Everything was okay without you. Had to go stick your ugly nose in where it didn't belong. This will be the last time you ruin my plans."

The threat froze Tenny's blood, but then, out of the dark, a high-pitched animalistic shriek sounded. The tip of the blade stung her cheek and neck. Shocked, her knees buckled and the hand holding her braid vanished as a flash of gray and black brushed by her. Precious! Tenny used the animal attack as an opportunity to escape, rolling to the steps, lurching to her feet, then running next door, screaming "Fire!" as she went. Uncle Mark believed people would respond to the word *fire* much more than the word *help* since fire meant everyone could be in danger. Her nearest neighbor, Belinda, switched on the porch light and cracked the front door. "Tenny? Where's the fire?"

Desperate for safety, Tenny scrambled up the steps and used her shoulder to push the door wider and wiggle in before answering. Gasping for breath, she faced Belinda, dressed in a rainbow fuzzy robe with pink, plaid pajama legs underneath and a head full of pink rollers. Tenny's heart was beating so hard it might just leave her chest—she placed one hand over it to prevent its sudden exit. "Yes, it's me. No fire. Call the sheriff!"

Shrieking and cursing came from outside, followed by the sound of a car door slamming and rubber burning as a vehicle left. Gone, at least for now. Tenny worked her way to the sofa and collapsed. Belinda hurried over, touching her cheek. "You're bleeding. Oh my. Your neck, too." She reached for a nearby tissue box and bunched a wad, placing it against Tenny's neck and cheek. "You hold onto these while I call."

Numb, Tenny did as told, clutching the tissues over her superficial wounds and realizing it could have been so much worse. She listened as Belinda reached the county sheriff, who handled several of the small towns without a law enforcement presence.

"My neighbor has been attacked."

Silence.

"I'm not sure what happened. She's bleeding. Neck and cheek. Lots of screaming, then a car took off." She glanced back at Tenny and angled her head, finally walking around to get a good look at her. "Mercy! They've gone and chopped off her hair."

Hair? Tenny's fingers moved over her scalp, finding a few strands of hair still half braided, but nothing else. A trickle slid down her neck, soaking into the collar of the white nightshirt already smeared with blood. Without Precious, it might have been more than her braid that had been cut. "Oh my!" She whispered the words. "I must have a guardian angel."

"You do." Belinda finished with the call, perched on the couch beside her, and wrapped her in a hug.

"I'd say it was Cinnamon and Mark who protected you tonight."

She leaned into the woman, enjoying the warmth and support. "Surprisingly, they used Precious to save my life."

"Precious?" The woman mumbled against her hair and then pulled back, regarding her with shock. "That flea-bitten raccoon Cinnamon made such a fuss over?"

"The same." Maybe she should go check on her four-footed rescuer. "I'd better check on him. He may have gotten hurt."

Gripping Tenny's arm tightly enough to leave a mark, Belinda shook her head. "Wait! You have no clue if there's someone out there waiting for you to pop your head out. I can wake my husband to check." She pressed her lips together and gave a small snort. "It would be better to wait for the sheriff. Besides, George isn't all that easy to wake up. It's more like disturbing a bear. Let the professionals handle it."

The phrase sounded familiar and made sense. All the same, she moved toward the front windows and pushed the curtains aside. The grass appeared gray in the moonlight and the concrete planters remained full of mums. Nothing different, except something small and black against the sidewalk. Not much she *could* do but wait.

The memory of the hissed threat arrived with an all-over shiver. Hate had filled the words. Even though she hadn't seen her attacker, she'd place money on whom it was. If she were in danger, others might be, too. "Belinda, I need to use your phone."

"Go ahead, honey. It's right over there. Do you have family I don't know about?"

Whatever she said on the landline would become fodder for the gossip hotline. "No. I need to call Blue. Would you know Moo Town's number?"

There was no need to ask if her neighbor knew Blue's cell number because she wouldn't. Belinda disappeared in the direction of the kitchen and returned clutching a cow-shaped magnet with Moo Town's number.

Thanking Belinda, she turned her body a bit as if that would block her conversation. She punched in the number and waited. It rang and rang. Could be the landline was only for use in the store or the milking barn. Finally, after six rings, a sleepy Griffin answered. "This better be important."

"It is. This is Tenny and I was just attacked at my house. I wanted to make sure the culprit wasn't on the way to your farm or possibly Dallas' house."

Griffin's voice went from drowsy to alert and he peppered her with questions. Well aware of her listening audience, she kept her answers short. "Yes, it is someone we know. In fact, someone who passed us on the road home yesterday. Blue will know. Can you contact Dallas?"

She waited for his affirmation before bidding him goodbye and hanging up. When she turned, Belinda folded her arms and murmured, "It's about time that gal gets her comeuppance, and maybe this time her parents won't be able to buy her way out of it."

The possibility of an even angrier Rita on the loose due to her parents' smoke and mirror machinations frightened her even more. Why couldn't things be tied up with a neat bow like her sixty-minute crime dramas?

THE MECHANICAL HUM of a truck drew Tenny to the window. Belinda joined her as they watched the parade of vehicles that must have met on the road into town. Moo Town's distinctive truck parked first, followed by Dallas, then the two-toned sheriff SUV. Blue threw herself out of the truck and headed for the crime scene. Certain that vital clues might be compromised, Tenny swung open Belinda's door and yelled, "Over here!"

Her neighbor pushed the door closed and clicked her tongue. "You can't go meeting folks in your nightshirt. Here, take my robe." She took off the fuzzy garment and passed it to Tenny. "You let them in. I'll get dressed and start the coffee."

No sooner had she tied the sash on the robe than a knock sounded. Tenny opened the door to both Blue and Dallas, who vied to get through the door first. They both entered talking.

"What happened?"

"Are you all right?"

"Your hair?"

"Is that blood on your neck?"

Griffin entered with the sheriff, a middle-aged, barrel-chested man she'd met on her missing bull mystery. He pointed outside. "Is your attacker still in the area?"

"That depends." Tenny grimaced, well aware she'd have to retell the incident. Dallas wrapped an arm around her waist and guided her to the sofa. He sat beside her and held her hand.

"Go on," the sheriff urged.

A dressed Belinda entered, sporting a misbuttoned flannel shirt, sweatpants, and house slippers. Her attention swiveled to the kitchen where the coffeemaker's hiss indicated brewing, and the drama unfolding in her living room. She pulled a straight-back chair closer to the action and sat, not willing to miss a word.

"I wonder if it started when I called the tip line about a suspect in the Rivertown's missing relocation funds," Tenny mused. "The woman kept making me repeat everything as if she didn't believe me. Those calls are supposed to be anonymous, but that doesn't mean the operator didn't recognize my voice."

Belinda leaned closer and rested her hand on her chin, while

Griffin stiffened up, grumbling, as details of the Rivertown trip surfaced. "You told me you were going to visit Aunt Hazel?"

"We did," Blue confirmed in a soft voice. "Just did a few things on the way. You know how I am."

"I should by now."

The sheriff kept her going back over sections of the room at Canine Stampede and asking for more details. Finally, he closed his notebook. "You figured out who stole the money just from those couple of things?"

"Let me clarify." Tenny cleared her throat. "This is my *opinion*. It's up to those with a higher paygrade to figure it out."

"They are," he assured. He held up his phone. "Let's get some photos of your neck and your shorn hair. Since dawn's here, we can also walk outside and see if we find anything."

Tenny complied, anxious to discover what the black spot on the sidewalk could be and Precious' location. After snapping several photos, including the long line of dried blood that pulled a spate of retribution possibilities from Dallas, the sheriff placed a hand on his shoulder. "Don't go off half-cocked. I'd hate to be arresting you next. Keep a cool head."

"You're right," Dallas half-heartedly agreed while Tenny entertained fantasies of the law finding Rita hiding out with Lloyd. Even now, they could be toasting each other with champagne and making plans for their move to a Caribbean island.

Outside, the sheriff donned a pair of blue latex gloves and retrieved evidence bags from his car. Tenny pointed to what had attracted her notice. Picking it up by the edge, the sheriff held up a single black leather glove. "Looks like a woman's glove."

"I can vouch for that," Dallas remarked with conviction. "It was the third pair of gloves I bought her when we were married. She kept making me take them back and get another pair because they didn't fit right. Yeah, I remember those gloves." He pointed to a design of a long stem rose near the thumb. "Said she wanted something fancy, but not garish. Apparently, I had issues with hitting the right balance."

They picked their way through the glass shards and a lone red, curly braid on the porch. The sheriff bagged it with an apology. "Sorry, it's evidence. You can have it back later."

"It's not as if I can glue it back on. Take whatever helps." Inside the house, they found the brick that broke the window with a very unpleasant message that read: *Leave now before it's too late. Dallas is my property.* After snapping a few photos from different angles, the sheriff pulled the message from under the rubber band and bagged it, talking to himself as he did so. "It's as if she's trying to be caught."

"You might think that," Blue interjected, "but up to now, no matter what she's done, there's been no consequences. It's all ego. She may not want Dallas for herself, but she's not going to let anyone else near him. What's hers is hers. Personally, I've always thought she had a vendetta against Tenny."

A derisive snort pierced the air as Tenny's eyes widened with disbelief. "I'll admit she's managed to be a rough patch in the road of life for me. Just never understood why, though."

"Could be," Dallas started with a croak in his voice, and then cleared his throat of the lingering emotion, "you were never intimidated by her."

"You're wrong there. Intimidated plenty. I went to college and then took a reference librarian job far away because I couldn't imagine living here alongside Queen Rita."

The sheriff echoed her. "Queen Rita, huh?"

"Trust me." Dallas managed a solemn look. "We've all had run-ins with Rita. Some of us hid our wounds a little better. I'd appreciate your nailing her on this."

"Tell you what. Let's see if I can get some help from the county CSI unit. I will need you to not clean up anything. Is that possible?"

"More than possible. I just need to change clothes." She gestured to the back of the house where her clothes were located.

"Circle around the debris spill—every shard can be a clue."

Easing around the mess, she made it to the bedroom and grabbed the clothing basics, her glasses, purse, and her phone. She picked up a hair tie but put it back down again since she had nothing to tie back. Dallas, Blue, and Tenny walked down the front steps, trying to walk on the edges of the steps. One of those doorbell cameras would have come in handy. It would be so nice to have some hard evidence.

Griffin waited next to his truck and pointed to the side driveway. Sitting on top of the bookmobile, a certain raccoon waited, playing with a glittering strand.

"Precious!" Tenny dashed to the bookmobile and stared up at her whiskered hero. The sound of a truck door slamming and footsteps brought Dallas next to her, brandishing a granola bar.

"Hey, buddy! This has your name on it." He slowly unwrapped the bar, gaining the raccoon's attention. The masked bandit padded over to the edge of the roof and watched Dallas before climbing down to accept his reward. In doing so, he dropped the silvery strand, which landed on the driveway.

The morning light caught the metallic sheen of a name necklace spelling out *Rita*.

Epilogue

THE OVERHEAD LIGHT fixture highlighted the pink line under Tenny's chin. It was hard to believe two months ago she'd almost died. Every time she thought about it, her heart skipped a beat, which is why she tried not to think about it. Her fingers tousled her red curls as she admired her new hairstyle in the mirror. Blue walked into the bedroom and waggled her brows comically, and then feigned primping by patting her own hair, which pulled a laugh from Tenny. "Stop it! I'm almost ready. I guess I want to look my best. With the bookmobile stop being so close to Rivertown, locals are going to come and gawk at us, ya know."

"Let them come." Blue tilted her chin up. "Who wouldn't want to get a glimpse of an extraordinary crime-solving duo?"

"Maybe." Tenny attached dangling book earrings to each ear. "As far as I can tell, we can't pat ourselves on the back too much. While we suspected Lloyd was the inside guy, we never suspected Marvin with his aw-shucks home-spun charm. Dallas, who has a cousin in law enforcement, heard Marvin and Lloyd aren't even related. They're both opportunistic criminals who thought they'd take their father-son act to smaller, more trusting locales. Who would have known he was a long-time money launderer?"

"Not me. What's up with that?" Blue shrugged her shoulders and sighed. "Marvin was rather good with the dogs, though."

After Tenny attached both earrings, she swiped her lips with a clear gloss before answering. "The secret of a good con is knowing enough to sound believable. He gave the impression he built the Canine Stampede from scratch. It turns out the building was already there. It used to be a Dalmatian rescue that had gone defunct. He just placed a sign on it and a new coat of paint on the exterior and he was in business. As for Lloyd, he was the inside man. He had enough fake references to get a bank job. He really did work with computers and helped with the ATM machines, too. Apparently, he helped move money physically and digitally. The influx of Rivertown's funds proved too big of a temptation."

"No one noticed?"

"Technically, it never left the bank. He simply moved it to bogus accounts he created, or at least, that is what the numbers showed. Now, the bank was never unduly alarmed since the amount of money it expected to be in its coffers, was. Lloyd used the bogus accounts along with the Canine Stampede account for laundering purposes. He also tucked away money he'd skimmed off stagnant accounts. As for the money taken from the relocation account, I heard it went toward buying the Canine Stampede, the sportscar, and possibly, squiring around Rita. I'm not sure what else he purchased. When they brought them in, Marvin swore he was off the criminal path and was making a new start with doggy daycare." Tenny grimaced, not sure what to believe, but the whole affair left a bad taste.

Blue's concerned face reflected in the mirror as she asked, "Will Rivertown get their money back?"

Good question. Tenny fluffed her hair, liking the way it fell in place. Who knew all she needed was a poodle groomer to handle her riotous curls, especially after Rita hacked off the majority of her hair? "Dallas heard from the sheriff that the assets, such as Canine Stampede, the sportscar, and even a four carat diamond ring Lloyd most likely bought for Rita, would be auctioned off."

Blue made a tsking sound. "Everyone knows auctions only bring a fraction of what an item is worth. That's why people go to auctions."

"Thought the same. The bank is insured for instances such as this, but the best thing is the government payments for the homes never reached the bank, yet. Seems it takes the government a long time to issue a check—and they hadn't."

"For once, being slow to pay turns out to be the better thing." They both laughed at the improbability as Tenny finished her primping.

"The money from the Go Fund Me account and state payout added up to over two million dollars." Her shoulders went up into a shrug. "As for that, we'll have to wait and see what happens. Surely, they'll get back some of it. I'm ready to go if you are."

The two of them meandered through the house and outside where Dallas waited on the front porch with Precious. He whistled as the two exited. "I have to say Isabelle, the dog groomer, did a great job on your hair. You look like a sexy elf."

"Thanks, I think." Tenny touched her ears to make certain they hadn't become pointed with the hair change. "I had my doubts about using a poodle groomer, but she really knows curly hair. If nothing else good came from this case, I did meet Isabelle."

A masked face showed up behind the glider, chattered, and then boosted itself up next to Dallas. Instead of making a biting comment about the raccoon, he smiled at it. "I thought I'd take Precious back to the farm with me."

"Watch out for the chickens!" Tenny warned, not wanting to ruin this newfound friendship between the two males in her life.

"No worries. He knows the rules. If he's good, we'll go by the Dairy Bar and get ice cream. Peanut butter is his favorite."

"That's news to me. You treat him better than I do."

Dallas grinned and reached over to pet Precious. "He was here when I wasn't. Without Precious, you might not be with us."

"Don't forget," Blue added, "since Rita was bitten multiple times, and if it hadn't been for Rita's parents calling, asking if Precious had his shots, the law wouldn't have tracked her down, since her parents were intent on hiding her in a lakeside cabin." She held up her thumb and forefinger about an inch apart. "I feel a little sorry about her parents' going to jail for harboring a fugitive and obstructing justice, but the way I look at it, they enabled her to get away with hurting so many people for so long that it's fair they do time."

"Still." Tenny thought of how her aunt Cinnamon tried to see the best in people. "It was nice Rita's father sold me his property that we used for Emerson's Little Library."

"Nice, no." Blue stuck out her tongue. "He was trying to raise money for his defense. You're more like your aunt Cinnamon than you realize. Always finding the good in people."

Tenny blinked away a tear before wrapping her bestie in a tight hug. "That's probably the sweetest thing you could say. Not true, but I'm glad you think so."

The two stepped out of the embrace all smiles. Blue tucked her hands in her jeans back pockets. "So, is Emerson getting a library?"

"I'm betting the council will approve a library in its old location.

I'll probably run it Thursday through Sunday. I'll still run the bookmobile a few days a week, too. It might mean I'll have to cash in some more stocks to get started. I'm grateful for Uncle Mark's financial acumen and Aunt Cinnamon's thriftiness."

Dallas stood and draped his arms around Tenny, resting his chin on her head. "Make sure you leave a couple of days free for a social life. You're very important to me."

"I will," she promised, feeling safe, secure, and excited about the future. When he dropped his embrace, she took a step toward the steps. "The weather is supposed to peak at sixty-three with sun all day long. With Rita in prison for the next seven years, the worst that can happen is my card laminator might overheat, making so many library cards."

"Make sure to turn it off now and then. Isn't there an app you can use instead of actual cards?"

"Maybe." Tenny smiled as she strolled down the front step, still talking as she did so. "Why don't you look into that for me?"

Both Blue and Tenny waved as they climbed into the bookmobile and reversed down the driveway. They slowly went through town, waving at townspeople who came off their porches or out of their homes to acknowledge them. Tenny occasionally beeped the horn at children who gestured for her to do so.

"You're a regular celebrity," Blue teased. "All it took was surviving a stabbing attempt from a local diva, plus putting her behind bars."

Tenny honked and waved at another child before turning west. "The law put her behind bars. I do feel fortunate, though. Very few people live long enough to see Karma in action."

"Yeah, you got that right." Blue adjusted her visor and added, "I hear there's a movie company coming to town—something about a local mystery. Who knows? They might ask us to star in it."

Tenny crinkled her nose at the possibility. "Stranger things have happened."

Over at the Almost Home Café, Jess and Hazel stood surrounded by townsfolk who wanted to know the details of the Rivertown Fraud case, including Sally. Blue rolled down her window and called out to her relatives. "Ever find out what happened to those escaping Angus?"

"City kids," her aunt called back with smirk. "Thought they'd try their hand at cow tipping."

The surrounding folks laughed, possibly at the image of liquored-up teens trying to push over a thousand pound animal and thinking it would tolerate such behavior. Tenny found herself laughing, too, but not at the image of drunken high schoolers pushing on a cow, but at the memory that she used to be called city girl, too, not so long ago—and now she was just another happy soul mentioned on the Emerson welcome sign.

THE END

Frogs, Floods and Fraud Recipes

Lentil Soup with Sausage

Ingredients

- 2 tablespoon olive oil
- 12 ounces kielbasa, thinly sliced (about 2½ cups)
- 1 ½ cup finely chopped yellow onion (from 1 onion)
- 2 medium stalks of celery, halved lengthwise and thinly sliced (about 3/4 cup)
- 2 teaspoons finely chopped fresh rosemary, plus more for serving
- 2 cups lower-sodium vegetable broth
- 1 14.5-oz. can no-salt-added diced tomatoes
- 2 14-oz. cans of brown lentils, drained and rinsed
- ½ teaspoon kosher salt
- ¼ cup sour cream (optional)

Directions

1. Heat oil in a large saucepan or medium Dutch oven over medium. Add sausage; cook, flipping occasionally until browned in spots, about 6 minutes.
2. Stir in onion, celery, and rosemary. Cook, stirring often until slightly softened, about 5 minutes.
3. Stir in broth, tomatoes, lentils, and salt. Bring to a boil over high. Reduce heat to low; gently simmer, stirring once or twice, until flavors meld, about 15 minutes.
4. Divide soup among 4 bowls. Top each bowl with sour cream, if desired, and chopped rosemary.

Easy Loaded Baked Potato Casserole

Ingredients

- 10 Yukon Gold potatoes, peeled and halved
- 6 slices bacon
- 2 cups shredded Cheddar cheese, divided
- 1 cup evaporated milk
- 1 cup sliced green onions, divided
- ½ cup sour cream
- 1 teaspoon salt
- ½ teaspoon ground black pepper

Directions

1. Preheat the oven to 350 degrees F (175 degrees C). Lightly grease a 9x13-inch baking dish.
2. Place potatoes into a large pot and cover with salted water; bring to a boil. Reduce heat to medium-low and simmer until tender, about 20 minutes. Drain and return the potatoes to the pot to dry.
3. Meanwhile, arrange bacon in a large skillet and cook over medium-high heat, turning occasionally until evenly browned, about 10 minutes. Drain bacon on a paper towel-lined plate; crumble and set aside.
4. Combine 1 1/2 cups Cheddar cheese, evaporated milk, 1/2 cup green onions, sour cream, 1/2 of the crumbled bacon, salt, and black pepper in the pot with potatoes. Mash with a potato masher until creamy. Spread the mixture into the prepared baking dish.
5. Bake in the preheated oven for 25 minutes. Sprinkle with remaining Cheddar cheese, green onions, and bacon. Return to the oven and continue baking until the cheese is melted, about 5 minutes more.

Tater Tot Casserole

This Tater Tot casserole is a quick and easy dinner that everyone will love. Just four basic ingredients come together for this comforting dish.

Ingredients

- **Beef:** This tater tot casserole starts with ground beef cooked until it's brown and crumbly.
- **Canned soup:** A can of condensed cream of mushroom soup adds richness, creaminess, and flavor.
- **Seasonings:** This casserole is simply seasoned with salt and black pepper.
- **Tater tots:** Of course, you'll need frozen tater tots!
- **Cheese:** Shred your own Cheddar cheese for the most delicious results.

Directions

1. Cook the ground beef, then stir in the soup and seasonings.
2. Transfer the beef to a baking dish. Top with tater tots, then the cheese
3. Bake until the tots are golden brown

Grandma's Vegetable Soup

This vegetable soup recipe is so easy and so good. My grandma used to make it for us.

Prep Time:
20 mins

Cook Time:
1 hrs 5 mins

Total Time:
1 hrs 25 mins

Ingredients

- 1 pound ground beef
- 1 (46 ounce) can of tomato juice
- 2 potatoes, peeled and diced
- 2 carrots, chopped
- 1 onion, chopped
- 1 (14.5 ounces) can of green beans, undrained
- 1 (14 ounces) can whole kernel corn, undrained
- 1 pinch ground ginger, or more to taste
- salt and ground black pepper to taste

Directions

1. Gather ingredients.
2. Cook and stir ground beef in a hot saucepan over medium heat until browned and crumbly, 5 to 7 minutes.
3. Drain off the grease and pour in tomato juice.
4. Add potatoes, carrots, and onion, then pour in undrained green beans and corn. Season with ginger, salt, and pepper. Reduce the heat to low and simmer for 1 hour.

Easy Cake Mix Cookies

There's no reason to wipe out your pantry supplies when this effortless, 3-ingredient cookie recipe exists. Plus, the boxed cake mix yields the softest, fluffiest cookies that everyone will enjoy.

Active:
5 mins

Total:
20 mins

Yield:
Serves 18 (serving size: 1 cookie)

Ingredients

- 1 (15.25-oz.) box cake mix of your choice (such as chocolate or lemon)
- 2 large eggs
- ⅓ cup canola oil

Directions

1. Preheat oven to 350°F (325°F if using dark or coated pans). Stir together cake mix, eggs, and oil in a medium bowl to combine. Scoop 1 1/2 tablespoons portions of dough, spaced 2 inches apart, on 2 baking sheets lined with parchment paper.
2. Bake in preheated oven until lightly golden around the bottom, 10 to 12 minutes. Let stand on baking sheets for 3 minutes before removing to cool, or to enjoy warm.

Movies, Monsters, and Marmalade

Available Fall 2023

Chapter One

A LONG, BLACK-ENCLOSED trailer pulled by an oversized truck rumbled westward down the street. Using her flattened hand as an eye shield against the descending Indian Summer sun, Tenny watched the truck as it eased down Main street, before swinging into a wide turn. In a town as small as Emerson, everyone knew what vehicles each family owned—and no one owned a shiny, new trailer, especially with no lettering. Magnetic signs identified vehicles as belonging to certain farms or served as a low-budget business advertising. Besides, those who had trailers also had a few dents in them from being backed into or misjudging the distance themselves.

She blew out a long breath, then stretched, trying to survey her neighbors without being obvious. A few of the children had stopped riding their bikes and gazed in the direction of the departing truck. Dried leaves danced across the sidewalk while the breeze rattled leaves still staunchly holding onto their tree hosts. Screen doors slammed in a distance, a mother called her children home for dinner, and a dog barked. Not unusual for a late October afternoon.

Normally, as a bookmobile day, Tenny would have been set up at one of the bookmobile stops, suggesting books or highlighting upcoming events. Not today, though. A mechanical issue had canceled out her latest visit and Tenny used the free day as an opportunity for all those little errands such as putting the glass insert into the security door before the winter winds blew.

Too bad many items on her to-do list remained. The heavy groan of a semi paused her reflection as another unknown vehicle moved into view. Her next-door neighbor stepped outside and strolled closer, forcing some acknowledgment. Tenny waved. "Hey, Bev!"

"Hey, yourself!" The neighbor stopped beside Tenny.

Red wavy letters announced *Last Scream Productions* with the final *S* bleeding off the semi-trailer. Bev read the name aloud. "Final Scream. What do you think that means?"

As a fan of crime dramas, Tenny shuddered. Nothing good came to mind, but she sucked in her lips and swallowed the comment. Not too far behind the semi came a parade of oversized pick-ups and fifth-wheel campers. Most showed age with their dated exteriors, faded paint, and rusty trim. Townspeople flowed out of their houses and businesses lining the sidewalks as if spotting the circus. An excited murmur grew in volume as locals speculated.

"Must be a detour," someone concluded loudly with several others agreeing. Tenny found herself nodding, but not everyone accepted such a simple explanation.

"It's those folks from the next town. They're spying on us!"

Tenny closed her eyes and sighed. In a small town, not only did you recognize vehicles, you pretty much knew everyone's views, too—even if she preferred not to know. Especially when it came to

Clive. His wife joked there wasn't a conspiracy theory he didn't embrace.

A bystander pointed out that driving a bunch of noisy vehicles through town couldn't be cataloged as spying. Clive disagreed emphatically. Even though it might be construed as eavesdropping, Tenny half listened, wondering why anyone bothered reasoning with the man. That's a small town for you. Everything generally remained the same, except when it didn't.

The last shabby fifth wheeler bore a hand-lettered near the side door reading WARDROBE. The single word jotted her reference librarian mind. Lots of vehicles, seemingly together, headed in the same direction, a semi labeled *Last Scream Productions*, and a wardrobe trailer. "Must be a movie caravan."

"What!" Bev shouted the word and grabbed Tenny's arm. "What's this about a movie? Who would they shoot a movie here?"

Several conversations stopped and people shuffled closer. *Small town life, you gotta love it.* Tenny cleared her throat, making certain she didn't misspeak and cause a wild rumor to race across the county. No doubt gossip would gallop through social media with various Hollywood heartthrobs sightings at the Almost Café or the Feed and Seed store. Still, she'd make sure *she* wasn't the source. "They're probably not shooting here. It could be they just need atmosphere shots. They're probably headed to Parke County with their historic covered bridges."

Not more than an hour north sat thirty-one beautifully restored covered bridges spanning rivers and streams. Depending on the season, the water sometimes dwindled to a trickle rather than an actual waterway. Fists on her hips, Bev wrinkled her nose and said, "What kind of a movie would feature a covered bridge?"

"Bridges of Madison County," Tenny offered, naming one of her aunt's favorite movies.

Bev sniffed. "I should have known you'd come up with that one. They might be doing a remake with younger stars. Everyone's doing remakes nowadays. Movie folks," she spat the words, "can't come up with an original idea. Gotta steal from the past."

Nearby listeners relayed what little they had heard, similar to telephone gossip with the details changing a little bit in each retelling. By tomorrow, Hollywood would be relocating to the town of Emerson that barely boasted a thousand souls. "I doubt any company called Final Scream Productions makes tear-jerking romances."

"Probably not," Bev agreed and lifted one eyebrow. "I guess I shouldn't expect any movie hotties in town, either."

Not certain who consisted of a *movie hottie* in her middle-aged neighbor's eyes, Tenny shrugged. "Probably not. I should get back to my errands."

"Yeah," Bev agreed and nodded. "By the way, are you going to make some of your aunt's famous marmalade this year?"

The simple inquiry pierced her lazy day contentment, making her flinch. Aunt Cinnamon had served as a fixture in Emerson with her mouth-watering concoctions and personal anecdotes. Her demise shattered the way Tenny thought of herself. Sometimes, she forgot the loss of Cinnamon left a gaping hole in the community fabric—one people expected her to fill.

"Um..." she stalled, trying to think of a way of saying *no* while making it sound a bit friendlier. "Cooking isn't really my thing."

"You have her recipe, right?" Bev asked with an eyebrow arch.

"I have all of them." Before her death from cancer, her aunt made a point of giving her the much-coveted recipes.

"There you go!" Bev offered a smile. "So many people have standing orders for the marmalade. I wouldn't be surprised if the list isn't up to two hundred already."

"Bev," Tenny racked her brain with how she could be more emphatic without spoiling her relationship. "I could give *you* the recipe."

Laughter greeted this pronouncement. Bev shook her index finger at Tenny. "Your aunt would turn over in her grave if she knew non-family had her recipes."

Even though her aunt epitomized generosity in so many ways, her giving spirit stopped when it came to her prize-winning, much-praised recipes. "Yeah, you're right."

Tenny pushed a lock of her short, curly auburn hair behind her ear still battling with how to excuse herself from making jars of marmalade she didn't have the time or inclination to do. "I forgot why my aunt made marmalade."

"Really?" Bev clicked her tongue as if to shame Tenny for her forgetfulness. "Your aunt made around three dollars per jar profit, which all went back into the young literacy program that allowed the local primary school teachers to buy books for the classroom." Warming up to the subject, Bev placed one hand on her hip. "As a small county school, we don't get much money. Most of the funds vanish as soon as they arrive, usually into the coaches' or adminis-trator's pet projects. Teachers get nothing. I should know since my sister used to teach at our primary school until she retired and was grateful for the money Cinnamon raised."

Tenny pasted a forced smile all through the story, well aware halfway through it that she'd be making marmalade. Just another item to her ever lengthening to-do list.

A familiar truck with black and white Holstein spots pulled to a stop in front of Tenny's home. Bev bid her goodbye as Tenny's best friend, Blue, named for her eyes as opposed to her emotional state, exited the truck. The generously proportioned blonde dashed up to Tenny and gasped, "Guess who escaped from prison?"

Author Notes

People always wonder, where do plot ideas come from? In **Frogs, Floods, and Fraud**, my initial idea came from a real story or should I say, how it was told to me. The small Indiana town of Leavenworth so damaged by flood waters was demolished, then rebuilt on higher ground by the WPA (Works Progress Administration.) It was promoted as an act of both compassion and the determination of the human will. Read more about it here. If you happen to be reading a paperback book, then type this into your browser. https://collections.libraries.indiana.edu/lilly/exhibitions_legacy/wpa /leavenworth.html

As for money being stolen to repair the town, another town had its flood funds depleted. In that non-fictional incident, they knew who stole the money because he scooted out of town with the funds. The culprit in question left his family behind and vanished with his girlfriend.

Another real-life tidbit was the mention of bank employees skimming a little bit of money off each person's account before they took off into hiding. The local news reported each employee stole about 100,000 in 1978. That would be almost 500,000 today. This stuck in my mind more than the other tidbits because I had my first bank account where the felonious employees worked. It's no wonder

I could never balance my checkbook.

Ever had to write a big check for a home down payment and the bank or realtor allotted a few days for this to happen? The money you think you have in the bank isn't physically there. If anyone remembers *It's A Wonderful Life* movie, when there is a run on the bank and everyone wants to pull their money out, George gives out his own money to keep the bank afloat as he explains how the bank invests their customer's money to help the community. It made me realize you don't hear about many bank robberies anymore since there is more actual money in grocery stores.

Another informational morsel is the FDIC which ensures your money increased the amount to 250, 000 as opposed to the former 150,000. If the government owes you money, it can take a long time before you see it. (No surprise there.) Finally, Indiana is rich in limestone, calcite, pyrite, and dolomite.

Find out what's happening next by visiting the website

MKScottAuthor.com

Happy Reading.